*Monsieur Pamplemousse
and the Militant Midwives*

*Monsieur Pamplemousse
and the Militant Midwives*

Michael Bond

Allison & Busby Limited
13 Charlotte Mews
London W1T 4EJ
www.allisonandbusby.com

Hardcover published in Great Britain in 2006.
This paperback edition first published in 2007.

A CIP catalogue record for this book is available from
the British Library.

10 9 8 7 6 5 4 3 2

13-ISBN 978-0-7490-8027-3

The paper used for this Allison & Busby publication
has been produced from trees that have been legally sourced from
well-managed and credibly certified forests.

Printed and bound in the UK by
CPI Bookmarque, Croydon, CR0 4TD

MICHAEL BOND was born in Newbury, Berkshire in 1926 and started writing whilst serving in the army during the Second World War. In 1958 the first book featuring his most famous creation, Paddington Bear, was published and many stories of his adventures followed.

In 1983 he turned his hand to adult fiction and the detective cum *gastronome par excellence* Monsieur Pamplemousse was born, accompanied as always by his faithful bloodhound Pommes Frites.

Michael Bond was awarded an OBE in 1997 and in 2007 was made an Honorary Doctor of Letters by Reading University. He is married, with two grown-up children, and lives in London.

Available from
ALLISON & BUSBY

Riffling through a sheaf of papers, Monsieur Pamplemousse carefully set them down in front of him, studiously giving the button to his right a wide berth as instructed by the Funeral Director. Not only was it set in brass, but it was clearly marked N'Y TOUCHEZ PAS! in large red letters. There was no point in taking any chances, particularly on such a solemn occasion as the one that lay ahead.

Having arranged everything to his liking, he placed his right hand on his heart, held it there for a moment or two while the congregation settled, then grasped both sides of the lectern in a business-like manner.

In truth, it was a purely theatrical gesture, for he had rehearsed what he had to say not once, but many times over during the past few days. Notes were superfluous; a kind of a belt and braces safety measure in case of trouble, and one he hoped he wouldn't have need to fall back on.

All the same, it served one useful purpose; it afforded the opportunity to get the feel of the assembly.

Par exemple: would some of the witticisms with which he had leavened his address while rehearsing it on the balcony outside his seventh-floor Paris apartment sound apposite in the more down-to-earth precincts of a crematorium, or would they strike the wrong note, falling on ground every bit as stony as that on which the chapel itself had been built?

He recognised many of the faces in the packed chapel.

Even though the service was taking place some miles outside Paris, the city's vice squad was there in force. That was only to be expected, of course; before moving on to higher things, Gaston Lefarge had been a leading light in the Brigade Mondaine. Like himself, a bit of a loner, for a while their careers had followed parallel paths. Both had been considered 'loose cannons', liable to buck the rule book from time to time in the pursuit of justice.

They had first met up during Monsieur Pamplemousse's attachment to the food fraud squad: the then 200-strong section of the Paris police, whose task it was to search out run-of-the-mill farm chicken credited with having been born and brought up in Bresse and priced accordingly; scales with doctored weights; croissants made with margarine rather than butter; truffled *foie gras* containing Moroccan whites dyed black; there was no end to people's ingenuity when it came to passing off. The Brigade had done for food what the Musée de Contrefaçion had done for labelling and other forms of deceit: brought them to the attention of the public.

But other sections of the Paris *Sûreté*, including the Brigade Criminale, were also well represented, and what was perhaps even more rewarding was the number of brass hats in attendance. It was a tribute to Gaston's popularity.

The grounds outside had been packed with official cars when he arrived, the drivers either dozing at the wheel or standing around in small groups while they enjoyed a quiet smoke and a chat.

It was a catholic gathering and no mistake. At one point on the way in to the chapel he even thought he'd caught a glimpse of his boss's erstwhile au pair, Elsie, although what possible reason she could have for being there, or indeed what interpretation Monsieur Leclercq would have placed on it, was beyond him.

He couldn't help reflecting that had he known, Gaston wouldn't have been entirely displeased at the turnout; very much the reverse in fact.

On the down side, word must surely have got around. Any member of the local criminal fraternity with half an eye on the main chance couldn't help but be aware of what was taking place and would have lost no time in passing the information on to their colleagues in the capital. News travelled fast and in keeping with the times, coded emails would be flashing their way to the metropolis; mobiles working overtime relaying text messages. There must be many in the milieu who would be taking full advantage of the situation.

There were a number of faces Monsieur Pamplemousse didn't recognise. His erstwhile colleague had been born into a farming community and clearly a sizeable contingent of friends and relations had turned up to pay their last respects: ladies with their freshly coiffed hair held firmly in place beneath hats that probably only came out for funerals; the menfolk in their Sunday best, collars freshly starched, black ties knotted within an inch of the wearer's life, leaving them red-faced and ill at ease.

They didn't know how lucky they were. Compared with Paris it was relatively cool. The capital had been like an oven for the past few weeks. Lying as it did in a virtual basin, hot air trapped by the surrounding hills had covered the city like a heavy blanket, making breathing difficult. In consequence the death rate of people suffering from asthma or dehydration had risen sharply, particularly among the very old. Every day the papers published the latest figure; in total it had grown to several thousand.

Even so, despite being out of the city, his hands felt unusually clammy and his throat had gone dry. He wished now he'd arranged for a glass of water to be set within easy reach. Preferably one laced with some suitable restorative to give it a bit of body; a quarter bottle of gin perhaps, or some local *eau de vie* wouldn't have gone amiss.

'We are gathered here today,' he began, 'to pay our heartfelt respects to the late Chief Inspector Gaston Lefarge.

'Gaston was a good man. One of the best. He was what one might in truth have called *un bon oeuf.*

'A good egg,' he added by way of explanation for the benefit of a small group of uniformed officers from across the Channel. Occupying almost the entire third pew to his left, they added an international flavour to the proceedings.

Glancing up in order to bestow a friendly nod in their direction, he registered a lone figure in civilian dress. To his surprise it was an old friend, and he wondered what on earth he was doing there. National security involving the higher echelons of government, rather than vice, was more in Mr Pickering's line. Although if he had been taxed on the point, Monsieur Pamplemousse would have had to admit there were times when the two became so inextricably mixed it was hard to tell them apart.

Typical, according to Mr Pickering, was the late King Edward VIII's predilection for what was known in certain circles as 'the Shanghai Grip'. His appetite once whetted, there had been no turning back; the course of history had been changed and over the years Mrs Simpson's lifestyle had reaped the benefit accordingly.

Resisting the temptation to wave, Monsieur Pamplemousse picked up the thread again.

'As a member of the Paris *Sûreté*, Gaston was unique. Not only was he totally incorruptible, he was as honest as the day is long, and that in an organisation where, if I may say so, and I speak as a past member, the days are sadly often all too short.'

Glancing up, he registered smiles of self-satisfaction from the UK contingent. Looking as though butter wouldn't melt in their mouths, they were nodding and preening themselves like a row of peacocks. Mr Pickering apart, *les Anglais* could be insufferably holier than thou when they chose.

Undeterred, Monsieur Pamplemousse continued. 'Gaston's powers of interrogation were second to none. In his never-ending search for the truth he brought a new meaning to the phrase 'throwing the book' at suspects.

'The fact that more often than not it was a leather-bound edition of the A–M section of the Paris telephone directory is beside the point.'

Crossing himself lest some heavenly censor should be recording his address for future reference, he paused for a laugh and didn't go unrewarded.

As the titters died away, he glanced round again and caught sight of several be-medalled bigwigs on the far side of the chapel. Meeting their stony gaze, it was clear they were registering disapproval rather than approbation. The combined furrowing of brows was reminiscent of the vast, freshly ploughed fields he and Pommes Frites had driven past on their way down that morning.

Reading between the lines the message was clear: thank your lucky stars, Pamplemousse, you are no longer in our employ. Further promotion would not be high on our combined agendas.

Had he worn contact lenses he would have followed the advice of another ex-colleague and removed them for the occasion.

Hastily excising a passing reference he had been about to make regarding the fact that the very first Paris Crime Squad had been formed by one François Vivacon, an ex-convict who went on to become its eventual head, he skipped a beat. All that had been in the days of Louis Philippe, the Citizen King. These things were interesting, but much water had flowed past the Palais de Justice and the quai des Orfèvres since then.

'Not only was Gaston a colleague of many years'

standing,' he continued, 'but if I may strike a personal note, during that time he became a very dear friend to many, myself included, which is one of the reasons why I have the signal honour to be addressing you all today. That, and the strange course of events which took place only a few nights ago. I refer, of course, to the way in which he met his maker.

'Chief Inspector Gaston Lefarge was a man in his prime, and to depart this world in such an unfortunate manner was indeed an unhappy turn of events. It was a shock to us all, and I know he will be sorely missed.

'There must be many who, over the years, have perished in a blizzard while attempting to cross an Arctic ice floe on foot, or been swept down a mountainside in the Alps; victim of an unforeseen avalanche. Perhaps even plunging to their death in a cable car when the wire on which it travelled snapped, as such wires do from time to time.

'But to have been submerged by a freak hailstorm in Paris on a summer's day in a year which is on record as being the hottest for over fifty years, is the stuff of which works of fiction are made. The fact that it was several days before the ice melted only rubs salt into his wounds, many of which are on record as having been caused by stones larger than golf balls. Larger, and in Gaston's case, twice as lethal.

'That he was destined to be found by another ex-member of the Paris *Sûreté* while he was out for a walk one night with his master – I refer, of course, to my faithful hound, Pommes Frites, by great good fortune holder of the Pierre Armand trophy for being sniffer dog of his year – was yet another twist of fate; a twist so bizarre it almost beggars belief.

'Truth, *mes amis*, is often stranger than fiction.'

Aware of a faint sob coming from nearby, he felt a pang of guilt as he caught sight of a figure in black only a few feet away from him. It was Denise, Lefarge's wife, her red-rimmed eyes clearly visible from behind a token veil as she clung to his every word. Beside her were two teenage children, a boy and a girl, although given their mode of dress it was hard to distinguish which was which. He admired the way they were coping with everything. It must be a difficult time for all concerned.

Even to his ears the story sounded a bit thin, but having been out to dinner with Doucette on the night in question he could certainly vouch for the intensity of the storm while it lasted.

As for the heat...*pâtissières* all over Paris had been struggling to maintain their dough at exactly the correct temperature, and despite constant watering, what little grass there was in the Parc Monceau now looked the colour of hay at harvest time. Girls had taken to flaunting bare midriffs with even greater abandon than usual, and despite picturing what his old mother would have had to say on the subject (Mark my words, they'll suffer for it when they get to my age!), he couldn't help but envy them.

It was partly because of the unremitting heat in their small kitchen on the slopes of Montmartre that he had decided to give his wife a treat and take her out to dinner that night. Given his work as an Inspector for *Le Guide*, France's oldest and best-loved gastronomic bible, dining out was a bit of a busman's holiday, which was why he had chosen to go further afield than usual; to the rue Surcouf in the 7th *arrondissement* and a little place he knew where they would be assured of a warm welcome. A welcome moreover, which would include Pommes Frites, if not from the resident cat, at least by Madame and her staff.

As always, it had been like entering a home from home. The familiar surroundings: the bar on the left just inside the door, the blue and white tiled floor, the tables with their spotlessly white linen coverings, the *banquettes* and the bent-wood chairs, the flowers and the familiar pictures on the wall, not to mention the little blackboard listing the day's specials and the brass plaque in one corner recording the fact that Inspector Maigret had once patronised the restaurant – an honour not given to many.

Sipping his *Kir vin blanc,* Monsieur Pamplemousse found himself wishing, as he so often had in the past, that all restaurants could be as welcoming. It would make his job that much easier. As for the food…it was the sort of cooking he remembered from his childhood.

They had just finished their first course – *terrine de volaille maison* – one of Madame's specialties, and a favourite of Pommes Frites too (he was particularly partial to the gherkins accompanying it; they were sweeter than usual and made a very satisfactory cracking sound as he bit into them), when the phone rang.

From his end of the conversation Monsieur Pamplemousse gathered that someone else from the 18th *arrondissement* wanted to book a table for later that evening.

He agreed with Doucette when she wondered if it was anyone they knew. It was, in truth, a small world and all things were possible. It was also, as is so often the way, although he didn't realise it at the time, the first of a series of coincidences that would multiply as the days went by.

Halfway through their *ris de veau*, and some way beyond the halfway mark on a bottle of Mazis-Chambertin, the phone went again. It was the same people who had rung only twenty minutes or so previously.

The waitress relayed the message through the open door to Madame in the kitchen. It seemed they were *désolés*, but they had to cancel their booking. They couldn't get out of the front door to their apartment building let alone reach their car.

Doucette wondered why. Monsieur Pamplemousse gave a shrug as he replenished their glasses, murmuring that in his opinion it was more than likely something better had come up. It happened all the time in the restaurant business. But at least it wasn't a 'no show'. That was the worst crime of all.

Having rounded off the evening with a generous portion of *tarte tatin* laced with *crème fraîche* from a bowl left on the table, goodbyes said, promises made to come back soon, cries of *bonne soirée* ringing in their ears, they had headed for home, following a route that took them across the Place de la Concorde – crowded as ever – and on up past the Gare St Lazare towards the Place de Clichy.

It was in the Place de Clichy that Monsieur Pamplemousse had his first intimation of there being something amiss. Normally on a Saturday night it was an area to avoid, but for once it was almost deserted and they were through it in no time at all.

Carrying on up the rue Caulaincourt, they passed Arnaud Larher's pâtisserie on their left, and Doucette, her mind still dwelling on their meal, announced that on the morrow she would brave the downhill and back up again journey between their home and the shop to buy some lemon tarts.

Monsieur Pamplemousse's mouth had watered at the thought. Larher's lemon tarts weren't simply the best in all Paris, they were out of this world. They positively melted in the mouth, leaving an exquisite aftertaste. The secret, so he had read, lay in baking the *petit sablé* pastry separately so that it retained its crunchiness, and brushing it with egg yolk immediately after it came out of the oven to seal it, before adding the lemon cream. But he was sure that was only half the story. Hard work and attention to detail played a large part too.

'I shouldn't bank on it,' he said gloomily.

'Why ever not?' said Doucette. 'I can phone ahead and make sure they keep some for me.'

Rounding a right hand bend halfway up the hill, Monsieur Pamplemousse pointed to the road ahead. 'That's why,' he said.

It was piled high on either side with hailstones. In the pale light from the street lamps they looked for all the world like heaps of giant white marbles.

It was *extraordinaire.* He had never seen anything quite like it before. It must have been a freak storm, and despite the heat the ice showed no sign of melting. It was no wonder the people who telephoned the restaurant had abandoned the idea of going out.

A number 80 *autobus* heading towards them in the middle of the road flashed its lights as a warning. Having pulled in to his right to let it go past, he then had difficulty setting off again.

A little further on, past the brow of the hill and going down the other side, he made to turn into the avenue Junot on the final lap of their journey, and having got into a slide, came to rest with the near side of his 2CV jammed against a wall of ice.

That was it! Enough was enough. He decided to call it a day and leave the car where it was until morning. Woe betide any meter maid who gave him a ticket in the meantime.

Pommes Frites eyed his surroundings gloomily as he clambered out through the roof. He'd been looking forward to his postprandial walk after they got home and he'd had a chance to slake his thirst. Now it was clearly out of the question.

All around them there were signs of the storm. It was

incroyable. There was no other word for it. Trees had been stripped of their leaves; in some places smaller ones were uprooted, lying on their sides as though having been plucked out of the ground by some giant hand.

Lights from the upper floors of surrounding buildings were on and people could be seen leaning out of their windows gesticulating to each other as they surveyed the damage.

Monsieur Pamplemousse took a deep breath as the montage of events flashed past in what can have amounted to only a split second or two in real time, but felt as though it had gone on forever.

He must pull himself together. It was incumbent upon him to do his best.

All in all he was pleased with his oration so far. It seemed to have gone down well. It had been his original intention to mention that there had been a small round hole in the middle of Gaston's forehead, but in the event that hadn't proved necessary. Clearly all those present had been entirely happy with his toned down version of what had taken place. Anyway, he'd had his orders not to say too much.

He was about to resume when…talk of the Devil…there was a momentary flash of light at the far end of the chapel, followed by a loud bang as the entrance door swung shut.

Heads turned, and following their gaze he saw the familiar figure of Pommes Frites hurrying down the aisle towards him. As always, there was a regal air about the way he carried himself, much like a Monarch of the Glen. It set him apart from other dogs, and a murmur went round the crematorium as the congregation followed his progress. A few, emboldened by hearing of the part he had played in finding Lefarge, and assuming it was yet another theatrical gesture on the part of his master, so far forget themselves as to applaud, but they were quickly silenced by those around them.

Thank goodness, thought Monsieur Pamplemousse, Doucette had attached a black ribbon to his collar before they left home. At the time he had considered it merely a token gesture, but clearly it hadn't passed unnoticed, and went some way towards mitigating what others obviously deemed an embarrassing intrusion.

He was on the point of reaching for his silent dog whistle, but he had left it too late. Pommes Frites had other things on his mind. He was wearing his purposeful expression. Clearly he was perturbed about something. Head held high, looking neither to the right nor to the left, he went past his master without so much as a blink of recognition and headed straight towards the coffin.

Having reached it, his forehead furrowed in much the same way as the brows belonging to the hierarchy in the front row that were now fastening their gimlet stares on the intruder rather than Monsieur Pamplemousse, he paused for a moment.

Then, for reasons best known to himself, having placed both front paws on the bier, he lifted the black drape with his nose and gave a sniff which must have been clearly heard at the back of the chapel.

Slowly withdrawing his head he raised it, and in doing so allowed the cloth to hang about him like a shroud, the silver decorations adding a biblical air, not unlike the work of some early Italian master. At the same time it revealed what appeared to be a carved wooden replica of the familiar shield with the words POLICE NATIONALE emblazed across the top, smaller versions of which normally appeared on the side of police vehicles.

Closing his eyes, Pommes Frites savoured the result of his investigation for a moment or two.

Such was his concentration he might well have been some

ancient sommelier contemplating the bouquet of a rare vintage wine, awarding marks to an 1870 Lafite perhaps, whilst comparing it to a Margaux of the same year, drawing from a memory bank honed over the years by the consumption of a century and a half of lesser vintages.

It would have been a brave soul indeed to have risked dropping a pin at that moment, for the chapel had gone so quiet the sound would have echoed round it like the proverbial sledgehammer.

So intense were Pommes Frites' thought processes, the whole congregation, which a moment before had been abuzz with mixed reactions to the scene being enacted before their eyes, now hardly dared draw breath as they awaited his verdict.

It wasn't long in coming.

The furrows on his brow deepened still further as he dealt with some new and unforeseen problem.

He knew what he'd witnessed in the car park when the coffin arrived and was left unattended for a short time while the bearers received their instructions. He also knew all too well what he had just smelt.

There was no immediate answer to the first. For the time being that would have to be put on what his master sometimes called 'the back burner'. Undoubtedly all would become clear in the end.

That being so, he decided to concentrate on the latest development, which in his humble opinion was, without a shadow of doubt, not only the more important of the two, but needed addressing without further delay. Time was of the essence.

Backing away from the coffin, he turned to face the congregation, then he opened his mouth and let rip with a series of warning barks; barks so loud and unexpected following the preceding silence that those who had the misfortune to be sitting in the first few pews were in imminent danger of collapsing onto their hassocks with shock.

Monsieur Pamplemousse, on the other hand, immediately recognised both the tone and the underlying urgency behind them. They spelt trouble with a capital T, and having at long last made contact with his whistle, he raised it to his lips.

Silent though it may have been as far as the congregation was concerned, the effect it had on Pommes Frites more than substantiated the manufacturer's claims as to its efficacy.

The shroud covering his head fell to the ground as he performed an about-turn. Having given a double-take when he spotted the source of the call to action, he headed towards his master as though his very life and the lives of all those around him depended on it.

Fearing the worst, Monsieur Pamplemousse instinctively grabbed hold of the lectern a split second before Pommes Frites cannoned into it. Holding on as tightly as he could as it rocked on its base he felt something cold and metallic under his right hand and realised to his horror that he had made contact with the very thing he had been at pains to avoid.

A gasp of horror rose from the congregation as the coffin slowly and inexorably began moving along its rails. Doors slid silently apart to allow it free passage, then, as it disappeared from view, just as silently came together again, bringing the service effectively to an end.

Pommes Frites, who in fairness was as surprised as anyone by what had happened, let out a howl of such baleful quality a shiver ran through the congregation, and those nearest to him, most of whom had only just recovered from their first shock, instinctively cowered back in their pews.

Slinking out of the chapel a few minutes later, hardly knowing which way to look, wishing the ground would open up and swallow them both, Monsieur Pamplemousse found himself accosted by one of the bigwigs; no less a person than the Chief Commissaire himself.

'A *débâcle*!' he boomed. 'A *débâcle*, the like of which I have never before encountered in the whole of my long career.'

'An unfortunate send-off,' agreed a smaller acolyte with a pencil moustache; a born 'yes-man' if ever Monsieur Pamplemousse had seen one. He disliked him on sight.

'How could you possibly have allowed it to happen?' continued the Commissaire. He glanced distastefully towards Pommes Frites, hovering discreetly on the sidelines. 'If that is your hound, he should have been suitably tethered.'

'I left him locked in my car, *Monsieur*.'

The Commissaire's lip curled. 'Are you telling me opening locked doors is another of his unhappy accomplishments?'

'With respect,' said Monsieur Pamplemousse defensively, 'during his time with the *Sûreté* Pommes Frites acquired many skills. If you peruse his records, you will find that not only was he a recipient of the Pierre Armand Golden Bone for being top sniffer dog of his year, he also attended a course on various means of escape including the ability to open doors. In any case, I had left the roof on my 2CV rolled back because of the heat...'

'That is no excuse,' broke in the acolyte.

'Yes! Yes!' The Commissaire, was clearly becoming impatient with his underling too. 'In most other respects your address was a model of all that it should have been. Save for a few unnecessary excursions into the realms of sick humour it struck exactly the right notes.'

'*Merci, Monsieur.*'

'Tell me…'

Monsieur Pamplemousse never did get to hear what he wished to know, for at that moment the air was rent by a muffled explosion and the last he saw of the Commissaire was the back of his head as it disappeared beneath a mound of hangers on.

Trained to protect their superior in moments of danger, they flung themselves on top of him with a gusto reminiscent of a rugby scrum during an International at the Stade de France. Arms and legs flew in all directions.

Fortunately, as far as he could make out during the brief time at his disposal, all the relative limbs remained attached to their rightful owners. But that was about all that could be said for certain, before a cloud of dust slowly descended on them all.

Chapter Two

In retrospect, when Monsieur Pamplemousse was asked to describe the moment, he remembered the explosion as being more of a flat bang, spreading shock waves in all directions from its epicentre somewhere inside the chapel. At the same time he was aware of a large hole appearing in one of the walls and the sky being full of birds. The eerie silence which followed was broken only by the patter of falling debris.

What it must have been like in the chapel itself was hard to imagine and his first thought had been for any staff who might be trapped inside, but to his relief a moment later he saw figures appearing one by one from behind some bushes. They looked as shaken by what had happened as did everyone else.

There was a surreal quality about the scene; it was not unlike a battlefield, where some unseen General had blown a whistle signalling half-time.

All around him dazed people were slowly clambering to their feet, retrieving hats, brushing themselves down. An alarm bell started to ring, somehow bringing everything back to reality again. A man near him gave a wry laugh and muttered something about shutting the stable door after the horse had bolted.

Only Pommes Frites looked relatively unshaken. Having been listening to the exchange of words between his master and the others with growing concern, pricking up his ears every time he heard his name mentioned, he was wearing his 'I could have told you so' expression.

He had known what he had known and events had proved him right. Had he not acted as he did, then half the hierarchy of the Paris police force would almost certainly have been blown to Kingdom Come along with a good few others, including both himself and his master.

As for Monsieur Pamplemousse, his evident satisfaction on Pommes Frites' behalf for the way he had performed was tempered with the certain knowledge that a fuse had been lit, one which would be hard to extinguish. How long a fuse it was and where it would lead to was anyone's guess, but one thing was certain: from now on there would be no going back.

'I am not of the Catholic persuasion,' said Mr Pickering, 'but if I were, I think I would be inclined to subscribe to that branch of it known as Jansenism. Correct me if I am wrong, but as I understand it they believe in predestination.'

Monsieur Pamplemousse avoided the other's gaze, partly because he was still in a slight state of shock himself, but also because it was a subject he would rather not dwell on for the time being.

His own and Mr Pickering's paths had crossed more than once, and over the years they had become firm friends. However, much as he liked and respected his opposite number, he wasn't always easy to read. As with many English people he had met over the years, Mr Pickering's speech was peppered with *non sequiturs* and it was as well to pause now and then in order to look carefully between the lines in case you missed some vital piece of information. Before committing himself, Monsieur Pamplemousse felt he would like to know why his friend had been at Gaston's funeral in the first place.

With that in mind he had suggested having lunch together before going their separate ways. He wondered whether the answer would come while they were perusing the menu or later on over coffee. In the event it wasn't long after they had started on the first course that Mr Pickering dipped a toe into the water.

'Take our meeting like this,' he said. 'The fact that you were reading the tribute…'

'It was always Gaston's wish that I should say a few words if anything untoward happened to him,' broke in Monsieur Pamplemousse. 'He would have done the same for me had the positions been reversed.'

'But surely it isn't as simple as that,' persisted Mr Pickering. 'There has to be some explanation over and above our get-together being merely the culmination of a whole series of extraordinary coincidences. That's what I mean about Jansenism.

'For example, who would have predicted a freak hailstorm in Paris on one of the hottest days of the year? Looking through the relevant press cuttings, certainly not the weather men.'

'They were taken by surprise like everyone else,' admitted Monsieur Pamplemousse, 'and it was very local. When Doucette and I left home that evening it didn't occur to either of us that we would need a coat. We were lucky to have escaped without a soaking.'

'Another thing…take Pommes Frites finding the body as he did.' Mr Pickering began ticking off the points one by one. 'Also the fact that Gaston had been in your neck of the woods that evening in the first place. As I understand it, he lives…lived on the other side of Paris…'

'That didn't stop us seeing each other from time to time,' said Monsieur Pamplemousse.

'Granted. But from all I gathered listening to your eulogy, you weren't expecting to see him the night of the storm…'

Monsieur Pamplemousse shrugged. 'We shall probably

never know. Perhaps it was simply a matter of chance that he happened to be in the area.' Reaching for a bottle of Muscadet he topped up their glasses.

'Besides, I might ask you the same question. What were you doing at the funeral?'

'Like ships at sea, our paths crossed from time to time, in much the same way as do yours and mine.' It was Mr Pickering's turn to hedge. 'Who would have thought a few days ago we would be sitting here having lunch together?' He helped himself, first of all to a second helping of herrings, then some sliced potatoes from open dishes that had been left on the table.

Monsieur Pamplemousse took the opportunity to follow suit.

Both were as fresh as could be; the herrings, plump and of the highest quality, must have rested in milk first of all to remove the saltiness. Arranged head to tail in a flat open dish, they had been cooked in a Dieppe style marinade of white wine and vinegar, along with sliced onions, carrots, peppercorns and coriander seeds. A bay leaf or two, some sprigs of thyme, and some olive oil completed the ensemble.

The potatoes, firmly fleshed and waxy – from the pale creamy colour and the distinctive flavour of chestnuts he judged them to be 'ratte' – were still warm, and the olive oil that had been sprinkled over them was again beyond reproach. The bread, too, tasted fresh and was clearly from the second baking of the day.

The restaurant had been the first likely looking one they had come across. The view through the window of red check tablecloths, gleaming copper pots and pans over the fireplace, sepia pictures of times past on the walls, had lured them in and they had not been disappointed. Despite the lateness of the hour, Madame welcomed them with open arms, bustling around like a mother hen, making sure they were comfortable.

He wished now he had thought to bring his notebook. The little bistro was a find and no mistake; worthy of a 'wrought iron table and chair' icon. Working as he did for *Le Guide*, France's premier restaurant bible, it was an unwritten rule that no Inspector should ever be without a notebook. But, as Mr Pickering had just said, who would have thought it?

In the normal course of events he would have said his goodbyes to everyone and been heading back to Paris by now. Apart from which, he was wearing his best suit and it lacked the special hidden pocket sewn into the right leg of his working clothes.

He would have to rely on memory.

'Now Gaston is no longer with us.' Mr Pickering broke into his deliberations. 'And if it hadn't been for Pommes Frites, a good many others would have joined him.'

'They do say that when people die their body fills with gas,' mused Monsieur Pamplemousse, anxious to move away from the subject. 'And it was several days before Gaston was found. As you well know, Pommes Frites is blessed with extrasensory perception when it comes to smelling things out. Besides, he probably wanted to pay his last respects.'

'Pull the other one,' said Mr Pickering. 'It's got bells on.'

'*Qu'est que c'est?*'

'Look, I know that Gaston had been shot.'

'You do?'

Mr Pickering nodded. 'Word gets around. It's one of the reasons why I'm over here. The story goes that it wasn't so much the scent that aroused Pommes Frites' interest as the colour of the ice around the spot where Gaston had fallen before being submerged by the hailstones.

'I also know he was on to something big. He didn't say what when we last spoke; it was all very hush, hush.'

'Big enough to warrant what happened back at the crematorium? You think the two events are connected?'

'They have to be. My guess is the whole thing was intended more in the nature of a statement. Don't play around with us – we mean business. It was a follow-up on the shooting of Gaston. He must have been on the trail of something in Montmartre and he paid the price.

'I'm not talking body smells – I'm talking extra Semtex perception. By my calculation, there must have been a fair old quantity of it in or on the coffin; more than enough to blow a hole in the wall of the crematorium. Did you take a close look? It's over a foot thick in places.

'I take it Gaston didn't make a habit of carrying that amount of explosive on his person, and even if he did, the funeral parlour would have been remarkably remiss not to come across it when they were laying him out.'

Monsieur Pamplemousse speared a chunk of herring and, having detached it from the whole, made play of busying himself by adding some onion and carrot to an already overlade fork.

'So you think Semtex?'

'Since Lockerbie it's been the current favourite. It's relatively easy to get hold of and has a good shelf life. It's malleable so it can be moulded to fit any situation. It's incredibly powerful for its weight. The original version had relatively little scent, so it used to be hard to detect. It even *looks* safe.

'There was a case recently of a Scottish couple who set out for a holiday in France and the wife, not trusting that foreign muck, took along a packet of frozen pastry, planning to make some chicken pie. The airport police came across her unattended rucksack, took the contents for Semtex, and blew it up. The controlled explosion was rather less spectacular than expected and the Scottish couple went without their pie.

'Forgetting basic questions like who was responsible for it, and why,' continued Mr Pickering, 'what do you think made Pommes Frites come into the church? He must have been on the trail of something.'

Monsieur Pamplemousse had been listening to the story with only half an ear. It reminded him of the insignia resting on top of the coffin. He wondered. It would be perfectly possible.

'Bloodhounds are like that,' he said. 'They have enormous determination. Once they pick up a scent they never give up – they can follow it for hours. Also, it doesn't have to be fresh. It can be many days old.'

Privately, he didn't think Pommes Frites *had* been following a trail. His sense of smell wasn't that good. At no time did he have his nose to the ground. His gaze had fastened on the coffin as soon as he entered the chapel.

'He seemed to be making a bee-line for the coffin,' said Mr Pickering, echoing his thoughts.

'One of their drawbacks,' said Monsieur Pamplemousse, 'is an abundance of loose skin. The folds sometimes restrict their vision so much they tend to bump into things by mistake.'

'That must have been how he came to collide with the lectern and indirectly caused the coffin to be sent on its way.'

'A lucky accident as it turned out,' said Monsieur Pamplemousse.

'They've started adding ethylene glycol nitrate to Semtex

to give it more smell,' said Mr Pickering. 'But if he hadn't picked up on the scent, I wonder if he saw something happen in the car park? When did the coffin get to the crematorium?'

Monsieur Pamplemousse ran through his arrival ahead of the others in order to confer with the Funeral Director. He remembered it being placed in position while they were talking inside the chapel and he was being shown the lectern.

'And Pommes Frites was still outside at that point?'

'He wasn't inside the chapel,' said Monsieur Pamplemousse. 'Put it that way. I left him in the car.'

'All of which points to the fact that the bomb must have been timed to go off at some arbitrary point during the service. It was only by a sheer miracle that because it was cut short and finished early we all escaped with our lives. We might have ended up alongside Gaston.

'Forgive me,' he added. 'One mustn't speak lightly about an old friend and colleague.

'It's a miracle there were no casualties. I gather the staff at the crematorium were equally surprised at the coffin's early arrival behind the scenes. They were all outside having a smoke. Taking a quick drag as we would say back home.'

He gazed down at the recumbent figure half under the table. 'I trust Pommes Frites' devotion to duty won't go unrecognised.'

Monsieur Pamplemousse gave another shrug. He couldn't helping thinking it would be if the Commissioner's acolyte had any say in the matter. It was a matter of some small satisfaction to him that he was clearly not alone in his dislike of the man. He had come off much the worst in the scrimmage outside the crematorium when the bomb went off. Others in the group had seized the opportunity to make a point or two with their boots while they were at it. Any self-respecting referee with his eye on the ball would have lost no time in reaching in his top pocket for some appropriate warning cards.

'The Commissioner said he would be recommending Pommes Frites for some kind of award. I am not sure what he has in mind.'

'Something more than a mere mention in dispatches, I trust,' said Mr Pickering. 'A bar to his Golden Bone perhaps?'

'To be honest,' said Monsieur Pamplemousse, 'he would be much happier with a real bone. He is currently particularly partial to knuckle of veal. They are getting more and more difficult to come by these days. Most of them go to restaurants where they boil them down for stock. By the time they have finished with them they are fit for neither man nor beast.'

Reaching down he administered a pat on the head. Pommes Frites, who had opened one eye at the mention of the word 'bone', opened the other and responded affectionately. He had been hoping his master wouldn't take too long over the first course. Herrings were not high on his mental shopping list of desirable comestibles and he could detect the unmistakable smell of *boeuf bourguignon* coming from the kitchen.

'There speaks the true French dog owner,' said Mr Pickering. 'To answer your question…'

'*Excusez-moi.*' Monsieur Pamplemousse withdrew a mobile from his trouser pocket.

Expecting a call from his wife, his heart sank when he realised it was a text message from Monsieur Leclercq, Director of *Le Guide*. It was short and to the point: '*ESTRAGON!* Return to base immediately. *Bonne journée.*'

'I am sorry.' He held up the screen for the other to see. 'It will have to wait until another time.'

'*Bonne journée*,' repeated Mr Pickering. 'You know, one of the things I love about your fellow countrymen is that in times of emergency you still retain your sense of politeness. We used to have it. Once upon a time, in 1871 to be precise, when the English explorer Henry Morton Stanley met Doctor Livingstone at Ujiji on Lake Tanganyika, he commemorated the historic occasion with the simple words "Doctor Livingstone, I presume". I fear things have gone downhill since then. It's every man for himself nowadays, and devil take the hindmost. You can stand outside Harrods all day holding the door open and no one even notices you're there, let alone bothers to say "thank you".'

He looked keenly at Monsieur Pamplemousse. 'Trouble back at the works, I assume? A little too much tarragon in the sauce somewhere or other?'

'Something like that,' said Monsieur Pamplemousse vaguely.

'That's another thing I admire about you French,' said Mr Pickering. 'Your sense of priorities in times of trouble. Any other nationality would have considered an over-abundance of a herb in the sauce small beer compared with what took place this morning.

'Having said that, I think if you don't mind I shall stay put and finish off this excellent meal.'

Monsieur Pamplemousse resisted the temptation to explain that '*Estragon*' was *Le Guide*'s code word for an emergency; one that was only to be used in exceptional circumstances. In simple terms it stood for 'Drop everything. Come at once'. There were no excuses.

Removing the napkin tucked into his collar he called for the bill, at the same time signalling Pommes Frites to his feet.

Mr Pickering rose too and held out his hand.

'That is very kind of you,' he said. 'I shall be heading for the Channel tunnel, but I have little doubt that we shall meet again soon. In the meantime I trust you will take good care of Pommes Frites. I know you always maintain he is well able to look after himself, but I strongly suspect he may have upset certain people today, or shall I say – a certain *body* of people, and he won't exactly be flavour of the month.

'I wouldn't want him to suffer the same fate as Rusik…'

'Rusik?' Monsieur Pamplemousse paused.

'Rusik was a Siamese cat,' said Mr Pickering. 'He belonged to a Russian acquaintance of mine who was stationed near the Caspian Sea for his pains. Among his many accomplishments, Rusik had a talent for sniffing out sturgeon and through that he ran foul of the Mafia, who were smuggling large quantities out of the country for the caviar. It's a £1 billion market these days.

'To cut a long story short, Rusik's olfactory powers proved to be his undoing. Shortly afterwards he was run down by a car, the victim of a contract killing. The final irony being that it was one of the very vehicles which had aroused his suspicions in the first place.'

It was a simple, but sobering story, and Monsieur Pamplemousse spent most of the long drive back to Paris mulling it over in his mind. One thing was certain; what was done was done and there was no going back on it. Mr Pickering's cautionary tale had taken place in a relatively lawless part of Russia and there was no reason to suppose it would be repeated elsewhere. Or was there?

Entering the vast Da Vinci underground car park beneath the Esplanade des Invalides, Monsieur Pamplemousse deposited his 2CV on Level 1, as near to the exit on the west side as possible. He checked the time on his Cupillard Rième wrist watch. They hadn't done badly; in all probability they were still ahead of the news about the morning's events.

Instinctively, he found himself looking around to make sure there were no figures lurking behind any of the pillars, but the area they were in was too well illuminated for that.

All the same, his mood communicated itself to Pommes Frites, who took it upon himself to carry out a quick survey of the other vehicles, any one of which might have provided a temporary hiding place. But he, too, drew a blank.

A blast of hot air hit them as they climbed the exit stairs and emerged into the daylight. Once again Monsíeur Pamplemousse looked around, first at the thin scattering of trees surrounding the exit, then towards a nearby clearing where the usual small group of men were playing *pétanque* beneath what little shade was afforded by the branches.

It was ridiculous, of course, but the very vastness of the esplanade somehow underlined his own and Pommes Frites' vulnerability, and despite the intense heat he felt a cold shiver run down his spine as he turned his back on the scene.

Pommes Frites was an unmistakably large target, and he would never forgive himself were he to be the unwitting cause of his friend and mentor coming to any harm.

Having said that, Pommes Frites clearly had no such qualms; he was much more interested in the boules.

Just lately Monsieur Pamplemousse had taken to carrying with him a set of balls Doucette had given him for Christmas. For some years he had been harbouring thoughts of joining the local club in Montmartre when the day finally arrived and he had to retire. Having no wish to be treated as a beginner, he'd begun practising whenever he had the opportunity.

Pommes Frites had given his master a magnet on a string for picking up the balls when he got really old and could no longer stoop, but that day was far away. In the meantime he was more than happy to do the job for him.

It was a satisfactory arrangement on both sides. As far as Pommes Frites was concerned, Monsieur Pamplemousse threw the boules and at a given signal he went to fetch them. In return, despite the need to give them a good rub down with the small towel no self-respecting player was ever without (it was against the rules to play with a wet boule), Monsieur Pamplemousse was more than happy to let him join in. It was good exercise.

Talking of exercise… Instead of going straight into *Le Guide*'s offices, Monsieur Pamplemousse headed towards the southern end of the esplanade. After the longish drive he suddenly felt the need to stretch his legs a little.

Reaching the Place des Invalides, he waited while a never-ending stream of tourists on bicycles went past. They were closely followed by a dozen or so figures on the latest American craze to hit Paris: Segways – two-wheeled scooter-like platforms propelled by tiny electric motors.

Gliding single file along the pavement at a uniform rate, looking neither to the right nor to the left, their helmets combined with their upright stance to make the riders look for all the world like robotic invaders from some alien planet. Oblivious to the traffic lights and the tooting of horns, probably because most of them were unable to stop in a hurry, they crossed the road, then disappeared up the rue de Grenelle in the general direction of the Eiffel Tower.

Doubling back down the rue Falbert, Monsieur Pamplemousse stopped outside a huge pair of anonymous wooden doors, withdrew a plastic card from an inside pocket, and applied it briefly to a metal plate set in the stone wall. There was an answering buzz and a moment later a small door let into one of the larger ones swung open to admit them.

Having at long last reached the comparative safety of *Le Guide*'s headquarters, he began to feel more cheerful as the door closed behind them. Even old Rambaud, the Gatekeeper, not exactly noted for being a bundle of laughs, looked friendlier than usual.

All the same, he didn't really begin to relax until they were safely inside the lift.

Exiting the lift on the seventh floor, wondering what lay in store for him, Monsieur Pamplemousse tapped on a door facing him, waited a beat, then opened it and went inside.

Expecting the usual warm welcome from the Director's secretary, he was disappointed to find the room unoccupied; in fact, not simply unoccupied, but despite the warmth of the day outside, there was a distinct chill in the air.

Pommes Frites noticed it too, and for a moment he stared mournfully at the empty chair behind the desk.

Assuming she was probably ensconced with her boss, Monsieur Pamplemousse carried on across the room and tapped gently on the door to the Director's inner sanctum. If the matter was urgent enough to warrant the use of *Le Guide*'s emergency codeword, there was no point in standing on ceremony.

Monsieur Leclercq must have been hovering on the other side, for the door swung open almost immediately.

Having first made sure his outer office was empty, he murmured something unintelligible and waved them in.

'*Pardon, Monsieur?*' Monsieur Pamplemousse cupped a hand over his ear.

'*Entrez,*' hissed the Director.

Trying to strike a jocular note, and mindful of Mr

Pickering's earlier anecdote, Monsieur Pamplemousse essayed a pleasantry in return: 'Doctor Livingstone, I presume?'

Monsieur Leclercq gave a start. 'Don't tell me they have changed the code word already, Pamplemousse!' he exclaimed.

It was Monsieur Pamplemousse's turn to look confused.

'They?' he repeated.

'How much do you already know of what is going on?' demanded the Director. 'Have you been primed?'

'I know a certain amount, *Monsieur*,' said Monsieur Pamplemousse cautiously. 'I am not sure how much that is, compared with the whole, or even how much it is when viewed as being a part of the whole. I only know about those things that affect me personally. You must forgive me. I was wearing the English explorer Henry Morton Stanley's hat for a moment. The one he was wearing on the banks of the Ujiji.'

'The banks of the Ujiji?' repeated Monsieur Leclercq. 'Matters are worse than I feared. Do I know this Stanley person? Why was I not told about him? Who is he working for?'

Monsieur Pamplemousse considered his response with care. 'Perhaps I should wait until Véronique returns to her office,' he began. 'In the circumstances, I thought...'

'Alas!' The Director calmed down. 'Véronique is no longer with us,' he said sombrely.

Monsieur Pamplemousse felt his blood run cold. 'She isn't...'

'Dead?' For a brief moment Monsieur Leclercq looked a broken man.

'No, Aristide, it is worse than that I fear. Far, far worse.

'At a time when I need a secretary more than ever, I have been left totally bereft! Véronique has walked out on me!'

Monsieur Pamplemousse could hardly believe his ears. 'Véronique has walked out on you, *Monsieur*?' he repeated. It didn't seem possible.

'Has she gone for good?'

'I sincerely hope not,' said Monsieur Leclercq. 'I don't know what I would do without her. My hope is that her absence is merely the result of a temporary aberration. I put it down to the hot weather, of course, but she swept out without even so much as an *au revoir* or a *quelle dommage*.

'The simple truth is she objected to having her handbag searched when she came in to work this morning. When I insisted, she announced she was leaving before I inflicted on her the final indignity of carrying out a strip search. Something, I can assure you, Aristide, I had no intention of doing.'

'With respect, *Monsieur*, perhaps you should have. Most women look on their *sac à main* as being private territory. In my experience it is a "no go" area. Many ladies I know would regard removing their clothes as being the lesser of two evils.'

'That may be true in the kind of circles you frequent, Pamplemousse,' said the Director, heading across the room towards his desk, 'but it is certainly not the case in mine.'

While his back was turned Monsieur Pamplemousse couldn't help but notice all the slatted blinds were drawn. He had never known such a thing to happen before. Monsieur Leclercq gained a great deal of pleasure from the panoramic view of Paris afforded by the enormous picture windows occupying three sides of his rooftop office. He was apt to spend much of his time gazing out at the world, or that part of it bounded by the *périphérique*; pinpointing the many restaurants whose names graced the pages of *Le Guide*, planning which ones might need a confirmatory visit. There was even a brass plate let into the stonework of the balcony wall indicating which establishments had been honoured with Stock Pot status.

Monsieur Pamplemousse also couldn't help being aware of the fact that the single lamp on the Director's desk had been turned to face the visitor's chair. Surely he wasn't about to be grilled?

Pommes Frites, who had been occupying the intervening time searching in vain for the water bowl which was invariably ready and waiting for him whenever he visited the Director's office, noticed it too, and having been caught in its beam, hurriedly sought refuge behind his master.

Monsieur Pamplemousse gave him a consoling pat. 'There, there,' he said. 'You mustn't count on these things.'

'Few things are certain in this life, Pamplemousse,' said Monsieur Leclercq, overhearing the remark as he arrived at his desk. 'In the present state of the world, nothing should be taken for granted. I trust he realises it is Véronique's responsibility, not mine.'

'We came as quickly as we could in response to your message,' said Monsieur Pamplemousse, 'but those of us who have no means of removing our outer cladding found the heat particularly enervating during the journey.'

'Hmmph.' The Director emitted a growl. 'I'm sorry to hear that. Particularly as from now on Pommes Frites must be kept in a constant state of readiness; all his faculties will need to be in peak condition in case they are required at short notice.'

While he was talking, he picked up a familiar-looking form and, in the manner of a conjuror seeking to impress his audience by making it vanish into thin air before their very eyes, held it up to a shaft of light infiltrating through a gap in the slatted blinds.

If that were indeed his intention, he was doomed to disappointment, and he eyed the document with increasing disfavour.

'First of all, Pamplemousse, without naming names, I have to tell you that a certain person who is responsible for our wellbeing is worried about you.'

'Matron has succumbed to the heat?' queried Monsieur Pamplemousse. 'She must be practically on her knees with half the staff suffering from dehydration.'

'No, Pamplemousse,' growled the Director, 'I do not mean Matron. I am referring to someone who must remain forever in the shadows, but who has the safe-keeping and security of the entire population of France very much at heart. It is an onerous enough task at the best of times, but it seems a copy of your P27 arrived on his desk this morning and he is less than happy.'

'My P27, *Monsieur*?'

'Yes, Pamplemousse, the form containing your personal details. He wishes to know the meaning of the word "myob".'

'Myob?' Monsieur Pamplemousse stared at the Director.

Monsieur Leclercq heaved a deep sigh. 'I do wish you wouldn't keep repeating everything I say, Aristide. It appears you have entered it under the heading of "religion". Teams of highly paid researchers are even now scanning their computer files wondering if it is, perhaps, peculiar to some obscure African tribe. So far they have drawn a blank.'

'I filled in the form when I first joined the company,' said Monsieur Pamplemousse primly. 'It is, in fact, against French law to ask the question.'

'Unfortunately,' said the Director, 'it must have escaped

my notice at the time. However, it has now become a matter of national security and the country cannot move forward until the matter has been resolved.'

'Mind your own business!'

The Director went purple in the face. 'How dare you, Pamplemousse!' he boomed.

'It is an acronym,' explained Monsieur Pamplemousse. 'Each letter of an acronym happens to be the first letter of a different word…'

'I am perfectly well aware of the meaning of the word acronym, Pamplemousse,' barked the Director. 'But what is myob an acronym of? That is the question.'

'I have just told you, *Monsieur* – Mind Your Own Business,' explained Monsieur Pamplemousse, as patiently as could. 'It happens to be a phrase much used by *les Anglais*, the acronym of which is myob.'

'*Les Anglais!*' The Director appeared to have difficulty in swallowing, as though his worst fears had been realised.

'It seemed a good idea at the time, *Monsieur,*' said Monsieur Pamplemousse lamely. 'I have an English friend, a Mr Pickering – funnily enough he was at the funeral this morning…'

'Ah,' said the Director, momentarily diverted. 'How did that go?'

Monsieur Pamplemousse felt tempted to say 'with a bang', but it was no time for levity. One thing was clear, however; news of what had taken place had yet to reach Monsieur Leclercq.

'Mr Pickering,' he continued, 'uses the word a great deal whenever he has a form to fill in, especially when the question infringes on what he regards as personal matters. I gather he found it very useful when he was in the army and had to state his religion. When pressed to explain it, he came up on the spur of the moment with what he thought was a suitable answer.

'Subsequently, whenever there was a church parade and the command came for any Mid-Yugoslavian Original Baptists to fall out he was the only one able to respond and for ever after he was left to his own devices. You can hardly march to a non-existent church all by yourself. It proved to be an unforeseen bonus.'

'I hope you are not suggesting I use the same explanation to the powers that be in France,' said the Director. 'Those in the higher echelons will treat it with the utmost suspicion. The fact that it is in English will make it even harder to accept.'

'Be that as it may,' said Monsieur Pamplemousse. 'It is Mr Pickering's opinion that while the first duty of any citizen must be to his country, a person's religion is his or her own business and no one else's, and I would agree with that.

'Our American cousins may wear their hearts on their sleeves, but there is something very fundamental in the way they bring their children up to revere the Stars and Stripes and reiterate their allegiance to it, hand on heart, at every opportunity, irrespective of their religious beliefs.'

'Hmmph!' The Director sought refuge in another grunt. He consulted a list on his desk. 'Before we go any further there is one other matter which needs investigation.'

'*Monsieur* wishes to know my mother's aunt's maiden name?'

'No, Pamplemousse, that will not be necessary, although once again it has to do with your P27. Under the heading "distinguishing features" you entered the fact that you have a mole on your right knee. I have been charged with ascertaining whether or not that is so.'

Monsieur Pamplemousse found himself mentally

counting up to ten. He couldn't help wondering what Dr Livingstone would have made of such a question all those years ago on the banks of the Ujiji. For two pins he would have joined the Director's secretary, wherever she was.

'In these troubled times, Aristide,' said the Director, sensing the other's hesitation, 'one cannot be too careful.'

'Perhaps *Monsieur* would like to check me for hidden weapons while he is at it,' said Monsieur Pamplemousse. 'I may have a nail file concealed about my person.'

Reluctantly he reached for his zip.

'There is no need to remove your outer garments, Pamplemousse,' said Monsieur Leclercq hastily. 'A cursory glance will be quite sufficient. Perhaps you could simply roll up the right trouser leg?'

Having glanced over his shoulder in order to make sure all the blinds were safely in place, he opened a drawer in his desk and produced a torch which he held aloft with a flourish between thumb and forefinger.

'I find this whole business distasteful enough as it is. I have been drawn into it much against my will, but our country is in peril. We are up against forces that will stop at nothing and there is an amber alert. I would ask Matron to perform the task but this whole operation must remain top secret.'

Following the beam of light, Pommes Frites joined forces with the Director, gazing with interest at his master's kneecap. There were times when there was no accounting for human behaviour. Unaware of what the problem might be, he wondered if a good lick would help, although he had tried once before to remove the spot and nothing had happened.

'Perhaps *Monsieur* would like to borrow my camera?' suggested Monsieur Pamplemousse.

'That will not be necessary, Pamplemousse,' said the Director stiffly. 'My word will be sufficient.'

'I hope the anonymous person, whoever he or she is, will be of the same mind,' said Monsieur Pamplemousse, as he set about tidying his person.

'We shall never know,' said the Director soberly, 'and I am not at liberty to ask. Suffice to say, he is second only to the President in terms of power.'

'I hope he doesn't ask to see Monsieur Chirac's distinguishing features next time they meet,' said Monsieur Pamplemousse. 'I would not care to be in his shoes if he does.'

Ignoring the remark, Monsieur Leclercq crossed to his drinks cupboard on the far side of the room. Opening the door of a small ice-box inside he removed a bottle of Gosset champagne and two glasses.

'I suggest a restorative is called for, Aristide,' he said.

From the angle at which he was holding the bottle, Monsieur Pamplemousse deduced it was by no means the first glass of the day.

Gazing up at the portrait of *Le Guide*'s founder on the wall above the cupboard, he couldn't help but feel Monsieur Hippolyte Duval's normally saturnine features would have looked even more forbidding had he still been alive and able to witness the current goings on.

'I will have the whole sorry business decisionised by tomorrow,' said Monsieur Leclercq, handing him one of the glasses.

Monsieur Pamplemousse pricked up his ears at the Americanism. It was usually a sign the Director had been in contact with someone from the other side of the Atlantic. At such times he was fond of peppering the conversation with the latest jargon.

He also liked nothing better than to lace it with references to what he called his 'contacts in the Higher Echelons' and his ability to pull strings when necessary, but clearly in this case the position was reversed; other people were pulling the Director's strings and he wasn't entirely happy with the situation. Given his other habit of playing his cards close to his chest, Monsieur Pamplemousse couldn't help wondering how many he possessed, or more to the point, when he would reveal his hand.

'Am I to assume that my P27 is the only reason you wished to see me, *Monsieur*?' he asked.

'I fear not, Pamplemousse. That would be blue-sky thinking on your part.'

There it was again!

Monsieur Leclercq motioned him to sit down at long last, and even went so far as to raise one of the blinds, letting in a stream of light.

'We live in troubled times, Aristide,' he said. 'Unrest is rife in the world. Terrorism is everywhere. Hence my having to make sure you are who you say you are. I trust you are not offended.'

'I doubt if the people we are up against go through the same rigmarole,' said Monsieur Pamplemousse. 'In my experience many of them don't even know who their father was, let alone if he had any distinguishing features.'

'Countries of the so-called free world are surrounded on all sides by terrorism,' continued the Director. 'All nations have their soft underbelly. With America and 9/11, the twin towers, symbols of wealth and prosperity, were the target. Britain endured a similar attack on the London Underground railway. Russia continually finds itself embroiled with the Chechen rebels. In each case the enemy within strikes where it will hurt most. Over the years France has suffered at the hands of the Basque separatists…

'Now, the target is the very heart of France itself. Intelligence has word from a reliable source that a terrorist group is planning to inject poison into the food chain. What that poison is, or into what part of the chain it will be injected, or even when it will happen, is not yet known.

'As a nation we are caught between two stools. On the one hand every precaution must be put in place to safeguard the population. On the other hand, in order to avoid the kind of panic that would do untold harm to the farming industry, it has been decided to avoid at all costs admitting there is the remotest possibility that such a thing could happen. For that reason alone the need for the utmost secrecy is paramount. Before you leave I must ask you to sign a document to that effect.

'In the meantime, in order to explore all possibilities, the powers that be are setting up a "think tank" made up of leading figures in the world of gastronomy. I have been asked to suggest a name to be part of that team, and your own immediately sprang to mind. Given your background and the time you spent with the food fraud squad before joining *Le Guide*, you are an ideal candidate.'

'When you say it is a reliable source, *Monsieur*…?'

'*Impeccable!*'

'And the others who are involved?'

'The British, for the sake of *Entente Cordiale*. And the Americans. I imagine you are familiar with the name Claye Beardmore…'

'Isn't that the person who runs a cookery website? He has invented some kind of diet for people want to lose weight. I believe it is all the rage. He also has a column which is syndicated worldwide.'

'Correct. Beardmore also happens to be a CIA agent. An

interesting case. Like many members of that ilk, Claye is what is known as a "sleeper". Mostly they remain anonymous, leading a normal life – a garage owner here – a small shopkeeper there – until such time as they are called upon to serve.

'Unfortunately, what started off as a relatively low-key cover job caught on. In some respects you could say it back-fired. In short, it has become a worldwide success. The only saving grace is that since Claye's picture never appears on screen, anonymity is preserved.'

'The few pieces I have seen have always struck me as being very didactic,' said Monsieur Pamplemousse. 'Doucette finds some of the recipes depressing. A never-ending diet of raisins and rice is all very well if you have had the misfortune to suffer an arterial blockage, but there is little to recommend it otherwise.'

'Claye Beardmore is an extremely didactic person,' said the Director guardedly. 'What our American friends would call a tough cookie. And a very successful one at that.

'You must form your own judgements, but if you want my opinion Claye has been "downloaded" more times than you and I have had hot dinners.'

Monsieur Pamplemousse eyed the Director curiously. It was unusual for him to be on first name terms quite so early on in a relationship.

'You have already met, *Monsieur*?'

The Director hesitated. 'Briefly. Claye slipped into Paris late last night, ostensibly to take part in a recovery programme for food addiction. It is an occupational hazard. We rendezvoused and it was arranged that the two of you should meet up as soon as possible in order to exchange notes.

'I will give you the name of the hotel.' Reaching for a pad,

Monsieur Leclercq scribbled a name and held it up for viewing.

Monsieur Pamplemousse gave a whistle between his teeth. The Pommes d'Or was one of a small band of Paris hotels boasting a restaurant that not only had three Stock pots in *Le Guide*, but three rosettes in Michelin.

'It doesn't sound a very suitable choice for someone suffering from severe food addiction,' he said.

The Director held a match to the paper and watched it burn. 'It has the advantage of being very central,' he said enigmatically.

'When you get there go straight up to suite 704. I suggest you take Pommes Frites with you.'

Catching sight of Monsieur Pamplemousse's gloomy expression, he made haste to soften the blow. 'I would join you, but Claye wanted to see you in particular and three is a crowd.'

'It would be four with Pommes Frites,' said Monsieur Pamplemousse. 'Besides, he is not particularly partial to raisins, or fruit for that matter.'

Something in Monsieur Leclercq's avoidance of a straight answer set alarm bells ringing in his head. 'Do you not think, *Monsieur*,' he said, 'that a rendezvous with someone at a higher level than me would be more apposite?'

'No, I don't, Pamplemousse,' said the Director severely.

Avoiding the other's gaze, and clearly revelling in his new role, he busied himself sweeping the ashes into his waste bin.

'But since you have already met…'

Monsieur Leclercq ignored the interruption. 'Bear in mind, Aristide, that what you are doing isn't simply for *Le Guide*, it will be for France. I know you won't let our beloved Marianne down. I can only wish you *bonne chance*!

'Always remember, Claye Beardmore is a very influential person in the United States; arguably second only to Patricia Wells in the realm of food, and the world famous wine guru, Robert Parker. If we upset Claye, sales of *Le Guide* in America may suffer.

'And now, before you go I must ask you to sign the document I mentioned earlier. As far as the outside world is concerned, this meeting never took place…and that applies to any future activities too! From now on, secrecy is paramount.'

Having escorted Monsieur Pamplemousse and Pommes Frites to the door, Monsieur Leclercq hesitated, as though about to say more, then had second thoughts.

'Before you leave, Aristide, I strongly recommend you do up the zip on your trousers. And if you want my advice I should ensure it stays that way for as long as possible.'

For the time being at least, there was nothing more to be said.

Largely on account of a mass demonstration by Parisian motorcyclists over the installation of a second speed camera on the *Périphérique*, Monsieur Pamplemousse took rather longer to reach the Pommes d'Or hotel than he'd intended, but in fact it served him well.

It was early evening by the time he arrived there and the foyer was crowded. The reception desk was awash with new arrivals and their luggage; residents heading for a night out on the town vied for use of the revolving doors with outsiders arriving for dinner. Add in a private function or two for good measure and the confusion was such that his own and Pommes Frites' progress across the black and white marble floor to a bank of elevators on the far side failed to cause the raising of a single eyebrow.

Nor did the lift girl pass any comment as they entered her

domain. As far as she was concerned, bloodhounds weighing in at around forty-seven kilos wanting to use the lift might have been a daily occurrence. The hotel could be full of them.

It might well be the case, of course, reflected Monsieur Pamplemousse. Times changed. For all he knew, the Pommes d'Or could have joined the growing band of hotels who were suffering a drop in the tourist trade following what Americans referred to as '9/11'. Many establishments now offered four-legged residents special facilities provided they were accompanied by a bona fide master or mistress.

It was a reversal of what had been the generally accepted norm. Once upon a time it was the French who'd had a reputation for cosseting their pets and treating them as human beings, much to the disgust of visitors from across the Atlantic.

According to one of his colleagues, Truffert, who had contacts in America dating back to his time in the Merchant navy, the Starwoods hotel chain had set the ball rolling with its 'Love That Dog' programme. With an estimated canine population of over sixty-five million and a $31 billion pet product industry, dogs suddenly had a voice in the land and they wanted to be first in on the act.

Now France was following suit. He had read somewhere that the Trianon Palace at Versailles was offering a Heavenly Pets package deal where a pooch was able to share a de luxe double room with its owner and enjoy round the clock room service.

And it wasn't simply hotels that were cashing in. Dial 45 85 1274 and you reached Taxi Canine, which also ran a special ambulance service for *chiens*, perhaps aimed at those who had been living it up not wisely, but too well.

He wondered what the Pommes d'Or might have had on

offer to tickle Pommes Frites' fancy; a generous helping of *bœuf bourguignon* perhaps, to make up for the one he had been done out of at lunch time, followed by a scoop or two of vanilla ice cream? He should have checked beforehand.

'Suite 704?' he enquired of the girl as the lift doors opened.

'*A droit, Monsieur.*'

Although she didn't actually convert the movement into a sign of the cross, Monsieur Pamplemousse thought he detected a trace of animation as she gestured to her right. It was a classic case of eyes revealing what the lips concealed.

After the oppressive heat outside, the air-conditioned splendour within the hotel was something else again. The closely patterned carpet stretching ahead into seeming infinity wouldn't have disgraced the first class deck of an ocean liner (not that he'd ever been on one!). On the other hand, the doors on either side of the corridor were too widely spaced for that, indicating as they did the size of the apartments which must lie beyond. Another pointer was the stainless steel, sand-filled containers for cigarette butts situated between them; so vast and solid they wouldn't have looked out of place in the Place Vendome.

It was another world.

Any security cameras, and doubtless they existed, were well and truly hidden. He guessed that perhaps not all of the sprinkler heads let into the ceiling were quite what they appeared to be.

A little way along the corridor they met a page escorting not one, but two immaculately coifed poodles on separate leashes. Heads held high, all three passed by without so much as a glance in their direction, leaving Monsieur Pamplemousse feeling aggrieved on Pommes Frites' behalf.

Stopping outside 704, he pressed a discreet button let

into the wall, wondering as he did so what lay before him. In his experience, the world of espionage was very much a closed shop. Members of the faceless coterie made their own rules and there was no such thing as 'the norm'.

The Director had given little or no indication of what to expect; rather the reverse. He'd been unusually cagey on the subject, and had Monsieur Pamplemousse been asked to hazard a guess at which of the many possibilities it would turn out to be, he doubted if he would have come anywhere near the truth.

The last thing he expected to be confronted by when the door swung open was an old lady clutching a Zimmer frame.

Chapter Four

The woman framed in the doorway had what appeared to be the contents of a large fruit bowl dangling from a chain round her neck. The second item which also stuck out a mile, contrasting strangely with a floor-length ball gown that looked as though it might have been worn by Margaret Dumont in an early Marx Brothers film, was a state-of-the-art, diamond-encrusted Harry Winston watch with an alligator band.

The whole was topped by a luxuriant mop of blue hair reminiscent of a beehive. It had to be a wig.

The total effect reminded Monsieur Pamplemousse of a plastic figurine for a wedding cake. He knew a shop near the Place de la République that specialised in just such saccharine concoctions, often with near-the-knuckle variations calculated to enliven any prenuptial stag party.

His heart sank. Monsieur Leclercq had said nothing about Claye having a mother, and for a moment or two he was lost for words.

'I was looking for a Monsieur Beardmore,' he said nervously. 'Monsieur Claye Beardmore. We have a meeting arranged. Perhaps you could tell him I am here.'

The woman gave a cackle. It began life several fathoms below her undeniably impressive cleavage. Somewhat disappointingly, although it took time, the sound that finally emerged after a tortuous journey was not unlike a pile of rusty nails landing on a tin roof. He hoped for her sake she was taking something for it.

'Boy! You're gonna need some telescope.'

Monsieur Pamplemousse stared at her. 'You mean…'

'How about pressing the flesh?' Letting go of the Zimmer frame with her right hand the woman held it out in a gesture of welcome. It felt cold to the touch; as icy cold as the coal black eyes, both of which seemed to be measuring him for size.

'The third Mr Beardmore and I are currently unravelling.'

'*Excusez-moi…*' Monsieur Pamplemousse tried to cover his confusion by removing his hand, but failed miserably in the attempt. Despite her advancing years, Mrs Beardmore had a vice-like grip.

At the same time he registered a voluminous handbag attached to the front rail of the frame, and for a brief moment he could have sworn he heard voices coming from it.

Reaching inside the bag with her other hand, the woman withdrew what appeared to be a can of Coca Cola. 'That's the trouble with getting older,' she said. 'You keep leaving things turned on.' She pressed the top of the tin with her thumb and the voices disappeared. 'You suffer from that?'

'Not yet…touch wood.'

'You will,' said Mrs Beardmore.

Monsieur Pamplemouse pulled a face. 'Claye is a very unusual name,' he ventured. 'For a…'

'For a girl?' She gave his hand a final squeeze before letting go. 'Men call me that because I'm like putty in their hands.

'As for my ex. I met Newt at a tree trimming party last Christmas, but he couldn't keep pace. He was a grade one serial groper, I give him that, but that's as far as it went. We stayed together through most of January. Then he started taking advantage, like wanting to outsource me for handling all his travel logistics, so I told him…if you can't stand the heat – get outa my bedroom and make your own travel arrangements.

'Where does that leave me? If he cares enough to book in with a behaviour modification specialist – and I tell him it still isn't too late – we can maybe meet up again for key holiday events. Otherwise, for the time being I guess I'm what you might call an empty nester.'

'That is one of the sad facts of life.' Monsieur Pamplemousse felt something was expected of him. 'People expect too much of others. Often more than they are able to give.'

'You can say that again.' Mrs Beardmore executed a shrug which threatened to produce a few windfalls from around her neck.

No lightweight – at a guess she must weigh in at around ninety kilos – and demonstrating remarkable acceleration from a standing start, she shot past him and opened the door. He was reminded of the Segways he'd seen earlier; then, as she leaned over to transfer a multi-lingual DO NOT DISTURB notice from the inner to the outer handle, of a pecking duck that once upon a time had been all the rage.

'Better safe than sorry,' she said, closing the door behind her.

Sliding the dead-bolt lock into place, she turned to face her guests. It all happened so quickly even Pommes Frites looked impressed.

Monsieur Pamplemousse found himself wondering if there were many power-assisted Zimmer frames on general sale, or whether hers had been made to order.

'It's a one-off,' said Claye, beating him to the question.

Executing a perfect 180-degree turn, she spearheaded the way through another door into the room beyond. Pommes Frites so far forgot himself as to sniff the air as she went past. Having done so, he snatched a quick backward glance at his master, making his meaning abundantly clear before padding on behind.

Monsieur Pamplemousse couldn't help but agree with his findings. Although he wasn't able to put a name to it, the thought struck him that the perfumed trail Claye left in her wake owed more to liberal doses of aftershave than to the lilies of any valley he had come across during his travels.

Bringing up the rear, he found himself in an area rather larger than his entire apartment in Montmartre. It radiated an air of refined elegance. Deep blue velvet curtains on two of the walls were tightly drawn, rendering the room to all intents and purposes virtually windowless. In consequence, only the light from several chandeliers suspended from the ceiling added a much-needed sparkle to the gold leaf adorning the Louis XVI-style furnishings. It was more a palace than a hotel.

A huge leather sofa, large enough to have taken up the whole of one wall in his living room, still left ample space for a desk with a fax machine and a top-of-the-range Dell laptop on one side of it, and a large plasma-screen Phillips television on the other. The laptop appeared to be open for business.

Over and above the splendour of the furnishings and the non-attributable oil paintings of scenes from a bygone age, there were enough flowers distributed around the room to open a shop. If Mrs Beardmore was keeping up a front to the world at large it must be costing someone a small fortune. Madame Grante in *Le Guide*'s accounts department would have a fit if she saw it. Her scissors would have been working overtime.

Claye waved expansively as she passed through into what he assumed must be the bedroom, leaving the door open behind her. 'Excuse me while I freshen up. I've been taking a decompression nap. Make yourself at home.'

Taking advantage of his hostess' temporary absence,

Monsieur Pamplemousse did as she suggested and set off on a voyage of exploration. On a table near one of the windows there was a box of chocolates; small but expensive looking, it bore a name he didn't recognise...Etienne Malfont et Fils.

Pommes Frites gave vent to a loud sneeze. Cocoa beans always had that effect on him. The darker the chocolate, the louder the sneeze.

On a glass-topped table in the centre of the room there was another, much larger cardboard box. The lid was open, revealing a quantity of circular objects. They looked as though they were covered in some kind of glue.

'Krispy Kreme doughnuts,' volunteered Claye as she flitted past the open doorway. 'Help yourself. You gotta great choice; Chocolate Iced Custard with or without Sprinkles, Dulce de Leche, Blueberry, Cinnamon Twist...you'll find a list inside the lid.

'If you're a virgin Krispy Kremer, I guess you should try Original Glazed.'

Taking a closer look inside the box, Monsieur Pamplemousse suppressed a shudder. Closer inspection revealed the fact that some of the contents already had tooth-sized bite marks.

He hoped it wasn't Mrs Beardmore's idea of *diner à deux*.

'Thank you,' he said, fearing the worst, 'but I think I would rather save myself for later.'

'Sounds a great idea to me.' Claye emitted another cackle. 'It's a free world. If you want some for home, let me have your address and I'll have them pouched right over. But I gotta warn you – they can be addictive.'

Monsieur Pamplemousse declined the offer. He couldn't begin to picture Doucette's face were she to be confronted by a box of doughnuts minus her husband. Pouch or no pouch, addictive or not, he hoped they would be a poor substitute. Nor, for the time being at least, did he want to reveal his address.

'Access the ice box if you wanna drink,' called Claye. 'You'll find it inside the bureau. There's a bowl of water alongside for the pooch. I ordered it up specially.'

Following his master across the room, Pommes Frites registered a blue and white china bowl on the floor. Having given an ornate pattern visible beneath the water a cursory glance, he turned on his heels, clearly treating it with the contempt he felt it deserved.

Meanwhile, Monsieur Pamplemousse was about to investigate the whereabouts of the refrigerator when he heard the door bell.

'That'll be room service,' called Claye. 'Can you see to the door? I'll be right out.'

Room service consisted of a large waiter pushing a very small trolley which, as far as Monsieur Pamplemousse could see, was bereft of anything remotely resembling food or drink. His heart sank as he stood back and watched while the man set to work.

Clearing away the box of doughnuts, he busied himself for a moment or two laying a snow-white cloth over the table. The hotel's insignia – a golden apple – symmetrically placed to his satisfaction, he then set about a minimalist arrangement of silver cutlery at opposite ends.

Placing two upright chairs in position, he opened a small cupboard door in the bottom half of the trolley and withdrew two domed plates. A strong smell of toasted cheese wafted Monsieur Pamplemousse's way as they were put in place, and his taste buds suffered a further nose dive.

Admittedly, had it been a choice between acting as Mrs Beardmore's escort for the evening in a crowded hotel restaurant, or risking all that might go with a meal *à deux* in her room, he would have been hard put to choose which was the lesser of two evils, but one by one the dreams he had been nourishing of the meal to come disappeared like so many will-o'-the-wisps.

Scanning the guides before leaving the office, he'd pictured toying with the Pommes d'Or's celebrated *Ravioles de foie gras*, followed by their equally well regarded *carré d'agneau*; both helped on their way, perhaps, with a bottle of what one guide called their seductive Volnay 1er cru 'Fremiets' from Annick Parent; a name new to him, and which he was anxious to try. The notion of rounding things off with a *Soufflé Grand Marnier* accompanied by a glass of Juracon Moelleux, both of which received honourable mentions in *Le Guide* (he detected Monsieur LeClercq's hand at work on that particular entry), received equally short shrift.

'One of my all time favourites,' Mrs Beardmore's voice materialised from somewhere just behind him as the waiter lifted the domes. 'Cheese on toast, Jamaican style.'

More than ever Monsieur Pamplemousse wished he'd stayed at home. Expecting he would arrive back hungry after his day in the country, Doucette had prepared a navarin of lamb. As a special treat she had ordered two lemon tarts from Larher to follow.

He turned to find Claye had changed into a shimmering white dress several sizes too small for her. The most you could say about it was the colour went with the white fishnet tights.

'I hear you use a Leica.'

'I do in my work,' said Monsieur Pamplemousse dubiously. 'But I'm afraid I don't have it with me. Why do you ask?'

'Because…' trilled Mrs Beardmore, striking a pose, one

hand behind her head. 'I'm camera ready.

'You know what they say…' She took her seat. 'You are what you eat.'

Recalling the box of half-eaten Krispy Kremes, Monsieur Pamplemousse couldn't help but reflect on the truth of the saying. On the other hand…who was he to pass judgement? How about all those meals, both good and bad, he consumed annually on behalf of *Le Guide*. What did that make him?

He caught the waiter's eye as the man backed out of the room with what could only be described as indecent haste. As with the lift girl, the look said it all. For a moment he felt tempted to follow him out, pleading some suddenly remembered urgent appointment. But he had left it too late. The man closed the door firmly, leaving him alone with Mrs Beardmore.

He gazed at the rapidly cooling object on his plate.

'I know what you're thinking,' said Claye. 'You're thinking how do I keep so young and slim with all those calories I got around me?'

It had been the last thing on Monsieur Pamplemousse's mind, but the question demanded an answer.

'Conducting,' said Clay. 'All you need is a CD of the Beethoven 9th. It beats having a work-out in the gym any day of the week. I like the Furtwangler version best. That guy really went for it. You ever seen a fat conductor? *And* you get to live to be a hundred.'

Wondering whether he should break the news that Wilhelm Furtwangler hadn't made it beyond sixty-eight, Monsieur Pamplemousse decided against it and applied his knife and fork to a corner of the toasted cheese, noting as he did so that the bread was wholegrain from Poilâine. His spirits rose; stone-milled wheat flour, seasoned with crystals of pure sea salt, leavened with natural yeast – it was a definite plus. Someone in the kitchen must be taking the whole thing seriously. Closing his eyes, he placed the portion delicately into his mouth.

In fact…he savoured the taste…it wasn't at all bad. In fact…it was surprisingly good.

He speared himself another portion, a larger one this time, and for a moment or two they both ate in relative silence; the crunching broken only by a loud belch from Mrs Beardmore.

The dish was, in fact, an example of what, given first class ingredients, a skilled chef could do with even such a mundane dish as cheese on toast. It made a mockery of the old adage that you couldn't make a silk purse out of a sow's ear.

Small wonder the Pommes d'Or's restaurant enjoyed three Stock Pots in *Le Guide*.

He also began to revise his opinion of his hostess. Perhaps she wasn't beyond the pale after all. It was perfectly true that the simplest of dishes were often the most rewarding. It was a favourite game he and his colleagues often played at the annual get-together. What would be their choice of dishes for a last meal on earth? The present one could certainly win a place as a starter on anyone's menu.

Detaching a portion of cheese from the bread, he held it up to his nose. 'Interestingly,' he said, 'this cheese is a Banon.'

'Yeah?' Mrs Beardmore felt in her bag and for a moment he wondered if he was to be treated to a musical accompaniment, but instead she withdrew a glass jar. 'You want my opinion? They can keep their banana cheese. It needs something over and above to give it a kick up the ass.'

Monsieur Pamplemousse decided to try again.

'Tell me,' he said, 'I am very interested. What makes them Jamaican style?'

'This!' Mrs Beardmore opened the jar and spooned a liberal dollop of mahogany coloured sauce onto the side of her plate. 'Vernon's Jerk Sauce. It's the real McCoy. I get it from the King of jerk himself. Nobody makes it better. He has a dispensary on West 29th Street, New York City. Never go anywhere without it.'

Monsieur Pamplemousse could scarcely believe his eyes. Already waves of the hot spice borne on a gentle breeze from the air conditioning assailed his nostrils. He reached for his handkerchief as his eyes started to water.

'Sure packs a wallop,' said Claye.

'Forgive my saying so,' said Monsieur Pamplemousse, 'but is it not a little extreme? You run the risk of masking the very flavours this particular cheese is famous for; flavours which are an integral part of the joy of its being. Banon comes from the Alps in Upper Provence, where lavender, thyme and other wild herbs grow thick on the ground. Banon itself has been there since the eleventh century, and the cheese they produce is made from the sweet curds of goats' milk – what are known as the *caillé doux*. When you buy it in the shops it comes in an airtight wrapping of dried chestnut leaves; five or six leaves for each cheese, which are then held together with raffia.

'There is a reason for everything,' he continued, warming to his subject. 'And the reason it is sold that way is because it has to be made in quantity while the weather is good and then preserved for the winter months when the goats are unable to provide milk. Because the chestnut leaves have a high tannin content, they impart a distinctive flavour.

'The locals,' he added hopefully, 'recommend that you accompany it with a glass of dry white wine…'

Realising that Mrs Beardmore had gone quiet, he broke off from his dissertation. Anyone who travelled the world armed to the teeth with jars of relish to take away the taste of foreign food probably had no wish to know such things.

'SNORE! SNORE!' said Claye. 'That's brain candy. Am I right or am I wrong? What are you? Some kind of food freak? You get off on curds or something, huh? Like you suffer from erectile dysfunction.'

Crossing to the door, she slid the dead-bolt lock back into place. 'Let's not talk *fromage*. You fancy some dessert before we get down to business?'

Given that the waiter had taken the trolley with him when he departed, an indication that there was nothing more to come, Monsieur Pamplemousse wondered what it could possibly be. He hoped it wasn't one of the half-eaten doughnuts.

Removing her necklace, Mrs Beardmore spread it out across the table. 'I got things that'll give you an even bigger kick than jerk sauce. In fact, you gotta choice of four.'

Opening a Victoria plum she shook out a tablet. 'For starters there's V for Viagra. Or, if you need something hotter still…' She flipped open a cherry. 'I got Cialis. According to the packet it came in it's good for thirty-six hours, but who's going to be counting?

'Then there's L for loganberries and Levitra. Last of all, I got something even better.' She picked up a raspberry and pressed it open. 'How about this? Rexxion. It's from the juice of a Mexican cactus. They don't come any hotter. I tried it out on Newt. The last I heard of him he was going so fast he got taken for a dust storm in Texas.'

'Lucky old Newt,' thought Monsieur Pamplemousse, mentally calculating the distance between the table and the door.

Admittedly he would be up against a power-assisted Zimmer frame, and there was the security catch to undo, but with Pommes Frites' help they might make it together.

'Some day,' he said, playing for time, 'you must tell me how you got to be a food writer. It is a highly specialised subject and you seem to have been very successful at it.'

'Do you have to be an astronaut to write about the moon?' asked Claye. 'It's a gas.'

Monsieur Pamplemousse felt tempted to say a few more taste buds might help to make such a book infinitely more exciting.

'Besides, you don't want to believe all you read, especially on the net.

'You know something, Aristide?' She leaned over towards him. 'I just love your aura.'

It wasn't the best news he'd had that day. Close to, under the direct light of one of the chandeliers, he could see the joins in his hostess's make-up. On the whole he preferred the part that came out of a jar.

'I tell you something else,' she continued. 'We have a mutual acquaintance.'

Monsieur Pamplemousse gave a start. He racked his brains, wondering who on earth it could be.

'The name Dorman ring any bells?'

'You know Mrs Van Dorman?' The part he'd played during her efforts to re-enact a gastronomic feast hosted by Alexandre Dumas while he was staying in Vichy prior to starting work on yet another sequel to *The Three Musketeers*, was something he would rather forget.

The thought of the story being bandied about in American gastronomic circles had to be another piece of bad news. It might even appear on Claye's website. Nothing was sacred these days. Even Michelin had suffered when one of their ex-staff threatened to write his memoirs exposing what went on behind the scenes. Sooner or later it was bound to reach the Director's ears.

'She rated you highly,' said Claye. 'I'd love it if you dressed up as d'Artagnan again like you did for her. You still got the outfit? It sounds like you had fun, even with your hands cuffed behind your back. Or, maybe especially with them that way.

'You know what your Oscar Wilde said: "The only way to get rid of temptation is to yield to it."'

'He wasn't actually one of ours,' said Monsieur Pamplemousse. 'He just happened to die while he was over here.'

'Yeah? You learn something new every day.'

'How did you get to know Mrs Van Dorman?'

'I make it my business to know these things,' said Claye. 'It's part of my job.'

Monsieur Pamplemousse rose to his feet. He'd had quite enough for one day. First the business with the exploding coffin, now this. He was fast reaching the end of his tether.

'To start with,' he said, gathering up the tablets. 'I have no need of these things, and even if I did I can assure you this is not the moment.

'In fact…' rising to his feet, he looked round the room. For a hotel which appeared to boast every convenience man could possibly wish for, it was surprisingly deficient in waste buckets. Perhaps the kind of guests they catered for didn't handle waste.

Seeing nothing remotely suitable near at hand, he dropped the tablets one by one into the water bowl where, in a series of plops, they sank like the proverbial stones.

'Bravo!'

As he turned he realised to his surprise that Mrs

Beardmore was standing without the aid of her frame. All of a sudden she appeared to have shed a few years.

'I love it when you're cross, Aristide. You don't mind if I call you Aristide?'

Moving to the sofa, she sat down. He waited to see how she ended up. Was it to be the swinging leg routine? Legs crossed, with the outer one pointing towards him indicating friendliness, or away from him indicating lack of trust? Or even, Heaven forbid, enticing; knees pressed together and feet splayed out sending a 'come hither' signal. In the event it was none of them. Perhaps she didn't bend that easily.

'Listen,' she gave the cushion next to her a pat. 'Come here. I like to know who I'm working with, that's all.'

Sensing that he had passed some kind of test, Monsieur Pamplemousse wasn't sure whether to feel pleased or sorry.

Pommes Frites, on the other hand, recognising the signs, seized the opportunity to go on a voyage of exploration. Following his nose, he went into the adjoining room. Being deprived of lunch was bad enough, but nobody had even thought to offer him any of the cheese on toast. It would have been better than nothing.

He was gone all of ten seconds. Following another bout of sneezing he came back into the room.

'You know what Lyndon Johnson used to say when he was President?' said Mrs Beardmore.

Monsieur Pamplemousse shook his head as he settled himself down a respectable distance away from her.

'"I never trust a man until I've got his pecker in my pocket".

'Me? I take the opposite line. I trust everyone so long as I get to cut the cards. You can't be too careful in this business.

'What gives with the Zimmer? It stops people getting in your hair. They see you coming towards them holding on to a frame, they keep out of your way in case you ask for help. Keep 'em guessing – that's my motto. Besides, they say things in front of you they wouldn't do otherwise, like they think you're deaf and dumb or something.

'Anyway, let's get down to business. We got things to talk about.'

Reaching across to the small table she picked up the box of chocolates.

'Try one of these. You're a food inspector. I'd like to know what you think of them.'

Monsieur Pamplemousse looked at the box first. Although the name was new to him he saw they had an address in Lyon; once upon a time the chocolate centre of France. As far as he knew only Bernachon of the big names was still going strong, dating back to the days when members of the dynasty travelled the world in search of the finest cocoa beans. Nowadays, more and more artisan *chocolatiers* simply assembled materials others had sourced.

There was a note inside, printed in gold copperplate.

'*In our never-ending search for perfection these creations are handmade from cocoa beans grown especially for us in the foothills of the Venezuelan Andes. No stone has been left unturned in our search for the finest ingredients that go to make up the fillings. Please note: In order to marry the exquisite tastes of the one with the other the flavour of the enrobing chocolate may vary.*'

It sounded like serious stuff.

'Chocolate has a lot in common with wine,' he said. 'First you smell it, then you look at the colour, then you taste it. Professional wine tasters spit it out before going on to the next. *Chocolatiers*, on the other hand, leave a small piece on their tongue to melt.'

He popped one of those on offer into his mouth.

'You think they'd make a good present?'

'I have no doubt of it,' said Monsieur Pamplemousse. 'They are, if I may say so, very French. That is to say they are dark and in every respect of the highest quality. That includes the raspberry filling in this particular one, which came through at the very end with an unbelievable freshness.'

Mrs Beardmore looked pleased. 'Irresistible, huh?'

She put the box back on the table and returned to the problem in hand.

'Tell me, what's the thinking on this side of the pond?'

Monsieur Pamplemousse hedged his bets. 'It's all happened so quickly…' he began. 'I didn't know about it myself until earlier today.'

'You know something? Back home the theory is if we're talking bin Laden or anyone connected with him it's going to happen on some kind of special occasion – maybe an anniversary of some kind, or a day of national celebration when everybody is off work and relaxed.'

'In America,' said Monsieur Pamplemousse thoughtfully, 'it would probably be on Thanksgiving Day when everyone is having their oven-ready turkey.'

'Like when the stars and stripes flag pops up to show it's ready?' said Claye. 'At the same time releasing a stream of gas. I've heard that one before.

'It could be the other extreme – like 9/11. Ever strike you 9/11 is the same number you dial in an emergency? It gets you Police, Fire, Ambulance. That give you any ideas?'

'In Britain they use 999,' said Monsieur Pamplemousse, thoughtfully. 'Whichever way you look at it, that date has been and gone.'

'We're not talking Britain,' Claye reminded him. 'Or the US. We're talking Europe.'

'Brussels tried to bring in 112 for the whole of Europe,' said Monsieur Pamplemousse, 'but it never really caught on in France. English motorists used it when they ran out of what they call "petrol", so we stick to our old ones. 17 for Police. 18 for Fire. 15 for Ambulance. It saves time.'

'Bang goes another theory,' said Claye. 'Why are you guys so different? I'm just throwing up balloons. The other big question is not just when, but how? Any ideas on that?'

'If it's in the food chain,' said Monsieur Pamplemousse thoughtfully, 'I suppose it could be seasonal. Something everyone rushes out to buy the moment it comes in.'

'How about truffles? When do they start? November? That's not so far away.'

'They're not for everyone,' said Monsieur Pamplemousse dubiously. 'They're too elitist.'

'Is that such a bad thing?' asked Claye. 'At least it would make sure they reached the movers and shakers of this world.'

'It doesn't have to be connected with bin Laden,' said Monsieur Pamplemousse, remembering the recent attempt to blackmail the French government by a group of unknown terrorists.

'Not everything has to do with Al-Qaeda. Other organisations are often all too eager to jump on the bandwagon. The worst thing Al-Qaeda did was to bring them out of the woodwork and make them more ambitious – to think big.'

He was thinking of AZF and the threat to plant explosives up and down the country's rail system. At the time no one knew what the letters stood for, or even whether it was an individual or a group, but the price for laying-off had been four million euros.

For a time it had seemed like something out of a James

Bond film, with demands for the government to land a helicopter on the roof of the Montparnasse Tower in Paris to show they were taking the threat seriously.

Ten thousand French rail workers had carried out an all-night search for bombs along the country's thirty-two thousand kilometres of track. Having drawn a blank, the blackmailer's bluff had been called, but it had been a nail-biting time.

Not long after that there had been the massive bomb attacks on the railways in Spain. Planted in backpacks and detonated by mobile phones, they had escaped detection until it was too late.

Al-Qaeda had claimed responsibility, but with an election just around the corner the government suspected their old Basque enemies Eta were behind them. Perhaps the two had got together. If it had been Eta it certainly backfired. When the election took place there was an overwhelming vote against anyone associated with them.

By the same token, it had made his own government think again. Following the Spanish affair, unease had spread like wildfire through Europe's train travelling public. And who could blame them? People with backpacks had become objects of suspicion.

He was about to enlarge on his theme when he felt a vibration in his trouser pocket. He took out his mobile. It was Monsieur Leclercq.

Edging further away from Mrs Beardmore, he pressed the earpiece hard against his head and cupped the other hand over the mouthpiece in case the Director was in a booming mode, but he needn't have worried.

'I was wondering if you are in an "*Estragon*" situation, Aristide,' hissed the voice at the other end.

'I am not in a position to answer the question,' said

Monsieur Pamplemousse carefully.

'Why is your voice all muffled, Pamplemousse?' Monsieur Leclercq's voice rose by several decibels. 'I trust you are not under the bedclothes with Mrs Beardmore already – a victim of what I believe is known as a "date-rape" drug!'

'No,' said Monsieur Pamplemousse. 'Rest assured, I am not. I will be with you as soon as I can.'

Surreptitiously pressing the OFF button, he added a few *non sequiturs* for good measure, before slipping the handset back into his pocket.

'Bad news?' asked Claye.

'I'm afraid I shall have to leave you.'

Monsieur Pamplemousse tried to keep the note of relief from his voice. He wasn't sure if he had entirely succeeded, but Mrs Beardmore was already on her feet.

'We'll catch up,' she said. 'We've made contact, that's the great thing. In the meantime your pooch had better have something for the journey.' Reaching for her plate, she placed it on the floor within licking distance.

Pommes Frites, who had been wearing his thoughtful expression following his return from the bedroom, jumped to his feet.

'You need a comfort break before you go?' asked Claye, addressing Monsieur Pamplemousse. 'The bathroom's on through. Help yourself.'

Monsieur Pamplemousse didn't feel the need, but he couldn't resist the chance to see around the rest of the suite while he was there.

As with the main room, the bedroom curtains were drawn – Claye must value her privacy. Alongside a king-size bed there was a Samsung Media Centre, with a mirror doubling as a television screen, and below that a mini bar.

Her night-clothes – a rather surprising set of neatly folded striped pyjamas – were already laid out, a small pile of cellophane wrapped sweets neatly arranged on top.

A quick glance behind a partially open sliding cupboard door revealed several sizeable items of luggage. He tried lifting one of the bags. It weighed a tonne. There was no doubt, when Americans travelled they took everything with them bar the kitchen sink.

The en-suite marble bathroom had a full complement of mirrors, hairdryers and the usual selection of freebie offerings along with two cordless telephones.

Claye must have brought along her own medicine chest. Walnut, with piano hinges, bearing the insignia Robern of Pennsylvania, it was standing on a table between two wash basins. Getting it out of the country couldn't have been easy; getting it back in again might be another matter. He guessed all things were possible if you were a CIA agent. It opened doors. Inside the chest it looked as though there were enough bottles and surgical instruments to deal with everything from a common cold to major surgery. At one point, taking his time while drying his hands, he thought he heard Pommes Frites coughing, but after a moment or two it stopped.

'You want the bad news first,' said Claye, when he got back into the room, 'or the red alert?'

'Tell me,' said Monsieur Pamplemousse, fearing the worst.

'The bad news is your pooch has gotten himself over-dosed on water. I guess it must have been the jerk sauce. He went for it like his mouth was on fire.'

Monsieur Pamplemousse stared at her. 'I do not under-stand. How can you overdose on water?'

'Easy, if it's full of tablets.' Claye pointed to the floor.

'Licked it dry.'

Registering the empty water bowl, Monsieur Pamplemousse looked around anxiously. 'Where is he?'

'Bingo!' Claye gestured towards the door. 'Now you've hit the real bad news.'

'Don't tell me you let him out…'

'You don't think I was going to stay in the same room with him do you? Not the way he was looking at me every time I bent over. You French have a word for humping?'

'*Culbuter*,' said Monsieur Pamplemousse. 'There are others…*Sauter…tomber…*'

'Yeah, well, I don't want to end up as a testimonial to any of those on the back of a packet…you know what I mean?

'One of us had to go. It was either him or me. No prizes for guessing who won!'

Monsieur Pamplemousse rushed across the room, slipped the security bolt, and flung the door open. He was just in time to see a Greyhound go past at speed without giving him so much as a second glance. It had its tail between its legs. Otherwise the corridor was empty, but from somewhere in the distance he heard a group of assorted dogs howling mournfully. None of them sounded remotely like Pommes Frites.

'See what I mean by red alert?' Claye came up behind him and thrust the box of Krispy Kremes into his hands. 'I guess some other pooch is having the smile wiped off its backside.'

'Pamplemousse…' Monsieur Leclercq eyed his subordinate wearily from behind his desk. 'Words fail me…'

'I am sorry to hear you say that, *Monsieur*.'

Risking the possibility that his head might receive a direct hit from a passing thunderbolt, Monsieur Pamplemousse managed to look suitably sympathetic.

Having prepared himself for a broadside, the Director's loss of speech, although doubtless only temporary, was the best news he'd had that morning.

One way or another he had spent a sleepless night.

Doucette had not been best pleased when he arrived back home with Pommes Frites the previous evening, both of them in need of sustenance, particularly as she had just finished clearing the table and packing everything away.

In the end he drew the short straw. Deprived of food for most of the day, his appetite sharpened for reasons that were not up for general discussion, Pommes Frites lost no time in polishing off the navarin of lamb. It hardly touched the side of his throat. One moment it was there, the next moment it had gone; lost beyond recall, although from the way he kept licking his lips, the taste was well worth savouring.

Doucette remained unmoved. 'If you've spent the entire evening in a hotel that prides itself on having a three Stock Pot restaurant,' she said, when he reproached her, 'and all you've had to eat is cheese on toast, that's your look-out. At least you've got a tongue in your head. Pommes Frites hasn't.'

'Only because he was lying on the kitchen floor with it hanging out for all to see,' had been his response. 'If you don't consider that making your meaning clear, I don't know what does.'

At which point Doucette pointed out that having allowed the meal to grow cold while she was waiting for them, she'd hardly had anything to eat either.

It set the tone for the rest of the evening.

Offers to share the Krispy Kremes to make up for the lack of any alternative fell on deaf ears, as did the suggestion she could have first go at the Cinnamon Twist.

The news that he had spent his entire time ensconced in a hotel apartment along with an elderly female bent on administering potency enhancing drugs, far from producing waves of sympathy, went down like a lead balloon.

'Since when have you needed tablets?' demanded Doucette, completely ignoring his plea that it only showed how hard he had fought against the very idea of his being unfaithful.

There were times when telling the truth was not always the best option. Pommes Frites' uninhibited snores outside the bedroom door that night kept them both awake, only adding fuel to the fire and leaving him in a catch-22 situation.

It was all to do with a lack of communication. He knew Doucette didn't really mean it. She always fretted when she felt his life was in some kind of danger, and not wishing to worry her, he had left her in the dark as to what was really going on. So far he hadn't dared mention Pommes Frites' own fall from grace. With luck she might never hear of it.

Rising early, he had been out to buy the morning papers, but even *Le Parisien*, not noted for being slow off the mark when it came to nosing out succulent titbits of news for its readers, hadn't picked up on the previous night's debacle at the Pommes d'Or, preferring instead to chronicle the alleged infidelities of a well-known tennis star.

Nor had there been any mention on the France Info radio

news channel. Public Relations must have gone into top gear with their whitewash brush.

Alongside everything else that was happening in the world, Pommes Frites' escapade was probably a very minor matter. But it wasn't over yet, and you never could tell. Summertime was traditionally the silly season for news, and once the *journaux* latched on to something it could get blown up out of all proportion.

But for the time being at least, life went on as usual.

Taking a short cut through the gardens in the Square Suzanne Buisson on his way down to the newsagent in rue Caulaincourt, the usual quota of health freaks had been in evidence. A man with his back to any passers-by, looking as impassive as the nearby statue of Saint Denis, was in exactly the same pose some ten minutes later when Monsieur Pamplemousse made his way back home.

The rotund uniformed lady, who as long as he could remember wandered around every morning flapping her arms in a desultory fashion, showed no discernible loss of weight. But then, who was to say what she would be like by now if she hadn't practised her art so assiduously?

'What happened to the code of secrecy, Aristide?' demanded Monsieur Leclercq, bringing him back down to earth.

Monsieur Pamplemousse bowed his head.

'As for Pommes Frites' behaviour…' The Director gazed down at the figure stretched out on the floor, but if he was expecting any kind of response he was doomed to disappointment. Registering the still empty outer office, along with the continued absence of a water bowl, and putting two and two together, Pommes Frites had decided to show his disapproval by opting out of things for the time being.

'Advertising to the whole world your presence at the Pommes d'Or in the way that he did…' continued the Director, 'I hardly know what to say. One only hopes the *Société Centrale pour l'Amélioration des Races de Chiens en France* don't get to hear about it. He is almost certain to be black-listed. I doubt if he will be allowed to offer his services as a prospective donor of spermatozoa for the foreseeable future.'

'I doubt if he could manage it even he wanted to,' said Monsieur Pamplemousse simply. 'Although, having said that, last night's affair doesn't seem to have been picked up by the media.'

Raising his hands ceiling-wards in a gesture of mute despair, Monsieur Leclercq held them aloft for a moment or two. Then he lowered them, brought the extended digits together to form a steeple, and began beating a measured tattoo with his thumbs.

'There is a very good reason for that, Pamplemousse,' he said, as though explaining matters to a small child. 'Something in your tone of voice when we spoke on the phone gave me cause for unease, and shortly afterwards I contacted the Pommes d'Or's head of security. At the time he was otherwise engaged. When he did eventually return my call, the reason became abundantly clear. He was also at pains to point out that everything which took place yesterday evening is preserved on DVD for future generations of dog owners as a salutary example of how *not* to let their charges behave in public. It may even be used as Exhibit "A" in court.

'The consequence of that last comment was I spent half the night discussing the matter with the hotel Manager, who had been called in specially to deal with a flood of complaints from the guests. Many of them, being of frail disposition, had taken to their beds while seeking legal advice from their attorneys back home. Attorneys, Pamplemousse, who earn their living by making the most of such situations. Satellites connecting the Pommes d'Or with the United States must have been glowing red hot in the night sky.

'Luckily, not wishing the news to get out lest its reputation in the eyes of American dog owners is ruined for ever more, the hotel have succumbed to pressure. Veterinary surgeons have been called in, and the management has announced that in the interests of preserving peace and goodwill they are prepared to meet all costs and settle out of court.

'I have to say that one of the things I emphasised in passing was that *Le Guide* is currently checking the ratings of all the major establishments in France, and what a pity it would be if the Pommes d'Or were to be downgraded and lose one or more of its Stock Pots.'

'It would indeed be a pity,' said Monsieur Pamplemousse. 'Their restaurant's cheese on toast is superb. I have seldom tasted better.'

Monsieur Leclercq stared at him for a full ten seconds. 'I hardly think cheese on toast merits inclusion in *Le Guide*'s recommendations for a three Stock Pot restaurant,' he said.

'I very much doubt if jet-setting gourmets will be flying in from all corners of the world simply to partake of a *croque monsieur*, however much we recommend it.'

'With respect, *Monsieur*, cheese on toast is nothing like a *croque monsieur*. In England it is known as Welsh rarebit.'

'They are a devious nation, the British,' said the Director. 'Nothing is what it seems. It is no wonder they make good spies. What is the difference, may I ask?'

'There are variations, of course,' said Monsieur

Pamplemousse, 'but the classic recipe for *croque monsieur* as given in *Larousse Gastronomique* consists of two slices of buttered bread with the crusts removed, filled with thin slices of Gruyère cheese and a slice of lean ham to form a sandwich. The whole is then lightly browned on both sides, either in butter in a frying pan or under a grill, sometimes in the latter case with the top having first received a coating of a Gruyère *béchamel* sauce.

'Cheese on toast, on the other hand, is simply what it sounds like. Many years ago there was a famous English lady by the name of Madame Beeton who produced a classic book on Household Management. She suggested melting the cheese by means of steam, then adding mustard and pepper before pouring it over the toast, after which it is browned by means of a salamander. She pointed out that it needs to be eaten very quickly before it congeals.'

Monsieur Leclercq gave a shudder. 'I do not wish to hear any more, Pamplemousse,' he said. 'It sounds to me like the kind of recipe which would find favour with any terrorists who were suffering from a lack of ideas.'

'The Pommes d'Or's dish only followed the latter recipe in principle,' persisted Monsieur Pamplemousse. 'As I said to Mrs Beardmore at the time, the quality of the ingredients – the Poilâine bread and the use of Banon cheese – made all the difference. Whoever was responsible had honed the dish to perfection.'

'It would take a lot more than that to convince me,' said the Director.

He brightened as a thought suddenly struck him. 'On the other hand, Aristide, you may have hit the proverbial nail on the head. It could prove to be a useful weapon. We can always threaten to include the recipe in our list of the hotel's top three dishes should they not toe the line. It is an admirable suggestion. It will be one up on Michelin.

'As it is they risk being struck off the Canine Club of France's list of recommended establishments. That, in turn, would mean we should be obliged to remove the icon indicating *chiens* are welcome from next year's edition of *Le Guide*.'

'Perhaps we could replace it with a dog rampant,' suggested Monsieur Pamplemousse.

Catching sight of the look on the Director's face, he made haste to spring to Pommes Frites' defence. 'It was hardly his fault, *Monsieur*.'

In as few words as possible he went over the events of the previous evening.

Monsieur Leclercq listened in silence as the tale unfolded. Despite everything he couldn't help but look impressed.

'You mean he swallowed *all* the pills in one go?' he said at last. 'It is no wonder they had an immediate effect.' He eyed Pommes Frites nervously. 'I trust it isn't long lasting.'

Monsieur Pamplemousse offered up his hands in the time-honoured answer to an impossible question.

'Why didn't you tell me Claye was a woman, *Monsieur*?' he said.

The Director had the grace to look momentarily discomfited. 'This whole cloak and dagger world of espionage is new to me, Aristide. On the one hand it is all about the gathering of information. On the other hand no one tells anyone *anything*. People talk, but they don't really exchange any worthwhile information for fear it may be wrong.'

'Espionage can be a very lonely business,' agreed Monsieur Pamplemousse. 'You are very much on your own.'

'That being the case,' said the Director. 'I felt you should be free to draw your own conclusions.

'Your sorry tale confirms my worst suspicions. That woman is a sex maniac. I trust you didn't fall victim to her wiles, Aristide?'

'Certainly not, *Monsieur.*'

'They do say one of the properties of such drugs is that victims often don't remember what took place,' mused the Director.

'How she came to be a member of the CIA I cannot understand. I suppose it takes all sorts. Mind you, Claye is not all bad. She actually gave me a book just before I left; a somewhat abstruse volume on the history of the North American Indians. I suppose it is the thought that counts.'

'America is a land of strange mixtures,' said Monsieur Pamplemousse simply. 'All things are possible. If you remember, the late head of the FBI, J Edgar Hoover, was well known for his outlandish proclivities. He lost no opportunity in practising them with all and sundry. People entering his office made sure they never turned their back on him.

'While he was in charge he managed to gather material on practically everyone who came within his sights. The files he built up over the years concerning people in high positions were legendary, and he had no hesitation in using the information at his disposal whenever it suited his purpose.'

'Another thing,' said the Director, going off on a tangent of his own. 'I suspected there was someone else in the apartment the night I was there. Now I am certain. A short time after we spoke I tried ringing you again to make sure you had left and when Mrs Beardmore answered I distinctly heard a male voice.'

'Perhaps it was coming from her radio,' suggested Monsieur Pamplemousse. 'She keeps it in her handbag. It looks like a can of Coca Cola.'

'Pamplemousse!' barked the Director. 'This is no time for levity. The voice apart, I say I suspected the presence of another person – a man – because the previous evening, having been entertained with more glasses of water than I have drunk for many a year, I had urgent need for a *pipi*.

'At Claye's suggestion, before leaving I availed myself of what she prosaically calls the "comfort station" and you may not believe this, but…' Monsieur Leclercq lowered his voice. 'When I put my hand out to raise the seat, it was already up!

'I tell you, I was glad to get out of her suite in one piece. Do you know what her last words to me were?'

Monsieur Pamplemousse shook his head. It was too early in the day for riddles.

'She questioned my libido. She told me she thought I was probably an under-achiever!' The Director sounded mortified by the experience. Clearly it had been the final indignity. 'I trust you won't repeat that to anyone, Aristide.'

'Of course not, *Monsieur*,' said Monsieur Pamplemousse, having already mentally earmarked it for the next staff get-together.

'Did you,' continued the Director, clearly anxious to change the subject, 'did you glean anything concrete from your meeting with Mrs Beardmore, other than the fact that her appetites are not confined to the world of the kitchen?'

'She seemed anxious to test a theory of hers that any attack when it comes might not be widespread; polluting the nation's drinking water, for example, or tampering with the bread supply. Such things would be hard to bring about on a grand scale anyway, and would be counter-productive in that they would alienate the population as a whole.

'She put forward the idea that it could be something more esoteric, something aimed at those in a position of power.

She mentioned in passing the fact that the truffle season is approaching…'

The Director went pale. '*Sacré bleu*! You realise what that would mean, Pamplemousse. Such a thing would strike at the very heart of the French establishment: politicians, captains of industry, the elite – all those in positions of power; the movers and shakers of this world.'

'Mrs Beardmore's very words, *Monsieur.*'

The Director rose to his feet and crossed to the window. Parting one of the slatted blinds, he stared out through the gap at the world beyond.

'This is worse than I pictured in my wildest dreams, Aristide. After such a dry summer there is bound to be a grave shortage of truffles. That, in turn, will undoubtedly sharpen demand at the beginning of the season.'

He turned abruptly. 'Did she offer any suggestions as to how it might be brought about?'

'No, *Monsieur.* We were in the middle of discussing it when your telephone call came through.'

'As you well know, Aristide, *maître d*'s have a habit of bringing truffles to the table in a large jar, holding it up to each individual in turn as they lift the lid so that guests can concentrate on the characteristically heady scent emitted by the *tuber melanosporum.* Suppose the jars themselves had been infiltrated with some kind of nerve gas? Diners would be falling like flies all around them.'

'Perhaps after the first two or three slumped over their table,' suggested Monsieur Pamplemousse, 'any *maître d*' worth his salt would suspect that something was amiss.'

Monsieur Leclercq chose to ignore the interruption. 'We must assume the worst scenario, Pamplemousse,' he said. 'At the very least, nasal organs could suffer irreparable damage. Besides, think of the harm it will do to the industry. The truffle hunters of France will be decimated. It could mean the end of civilisation as we know it. We must move fast.

'Whatever happens, these thoughts must not be communicated to the public at large.'

Monsieur Pamplemousse stared across the room at Monsieur Leclercq. There were times when the Director could be unbelievably self-centred. Also, he couldn't help feeling he was jumping the gun more than somewhat.

'It was only one possibility out of many,' he said. 'I suspect she was simply throwing up balloons to see how I would react. It could just as easily have been *escargots*. The garlic in *escargots bourguignon* would effectively mask the taste of practically any poison you care to name.'

If anything, Monsieur Leclercq went whiter still, like a man suddenly staring ruin in the face.

'Heaven forbid!' he exclaimed. 'Think of our logo, Pamplemousse. What would become of our two *escargots* rampant?'

'I imagine they would be laid out flat as though they'd had a dose of strychnine,' said Monsieur Pamplemousse unfeelingly.

'You could publish a special memorial edition of *Le Guide* showing two molluscs lying prone with a leg in the air as though they have both had a night out on the tiles,' he added hastily, endeavouring to pour oil on decidedly choppy waters. 'If it had a black border it might in time become a collector's item.'

'*Escargots* don't have legs!' boomed the Director.

'With respect, *Monsieur*, they have one in the front. They use it to pull themselves along.'

Monsieur Leclercq brushed the interruption to one side. 'It only serves to underline the urgency of the situation, Pamplemousse,' he exclaimed. 'We must concern ourselves, not with future possibilities, but with the immediate present.

'First of all, I suggest you return to the Pommes d'Or and see what can be done in the way of damage limitation. I have spoken to the head of security and he is awaiting your call.

'No doubt he will want to show you the film. I understand it doesn't make for happy viewing, but at least it will give you a better idea of what actually transpired. You must disassociate yourself as far as possible from Mrs Beardmore in case questions are asked. At all costs we must preserve her anonymity. As far as the hotel is concerned you were there in a professional capacity on behalf of *Le Guide*. I am aware that that in itself compromises our own anonymity, but in the circumstances it can't be helped.'

'That may not be easy,' mused Monsieur Pamplemousse. 'If they have Pommes Frites on DVD, they may well have me on it too.'

'That is for you to ascertain, Pamplemousse,' said the Director.

'I can hardly take Pommes Frites with me,' said Monsieur Pamplemousse. 'If you could possibly look after him while I am gone…'

Monsieur Leclercq gazed dubiously floorwards. 'I suppose you are right,' he said.

'It is unfortunate,' said Monsieur Pamplemousse, 'that Véronique is no longer with you…'

The Director was cheered by a sudden thought. 'Perhaps, Aristide, you could call her and explain the situation. That should do the trick. She will jump at the chance. She thinks the world of Pommes Frites, as we all do. She will know exactly what is required in the way of exercise and refuelling, *and* it will enable her to return without losing face.'

And without your losing face, too, if I do the dirty work, thought Monsieur Pamplemousse. 'Then I can leave him with you, *Monsieur*?' he asked out loud.

By way of an answer Monsieur Leclercq reached for a telephone, dialled a number and handed it to his subordinate.

'It is all yours, Pamplemousse,' he said.

André Bonnard, Head of Security at the Pommes d'Or, was clearly a man who had found his true vocation in life.

Well-built, fiftyish, hair greying at the temples, rimless glasses, dark grey T-shirt embroidered with an 'I love Microsoft' logo, he oozed *bonhomie* and technical expertise as he sat like a dedicated organist before a bank of monitors.

There were two other younger clones hovering in the background – both wearing identical T-shirts, but it was clearly Bonnard's patch.

On top of the console, standing out like a sore thumb in the midst of all the state-of-the-art equipment, was an open box of Krispy Kreme doughnuts.

Like a grown man who has bought his son a train set for Christmas so that he could play with it himself, Bonnard radiated unalloyed pleasure as he switched rapidly between various sources, producing in a matter of seconds a moving picture of what life in a big hotel was all about.

Assorted shots of the foyer gave way to pictures of corridors with staff going to and fro; waiters pushing breakfast trolleys, cleaners at work, maids armed with piles of laundry. Such domestic activity then gave way to more mundane behind-the-scene shots of everything, from the huge boiler room in the depths of the building to the delivery area at the back, where vans were coming and going, and finally on to the underground car park.

'We have automatic electronic registration of car number plates as they enter and leave,' said Bonnard proudly. 'And currently we're playing around with face-recognition technology. It's not perfect, but it's improving all the time.

'I tell you, everything needed for a surveillance society is already with us. The architecture in the way of hardware is in place and is increasing all the time. People who do their shopping in a *super marché* and have a loyalty card forget their purchases are all on record back at the works. It's getting so that in the not too distant future there will be CCTV cameras on every street corner.

'The UK is top of the league with a total of over four million – that's one for every fourteen of its inhabitants. It is theoretically possible for someone in London to go about their normal business, travel to the office, maybe do some shopping at lunch time, take in a football match in the evening, and end up the day having been on camera three hundred times or more. True, different cameras and different systems belong to different organisations, much like an unedited film, but put them all together and it's a sobering thought. It certainly proved its worth after last July's terrorist attack on the Underground.

'On the other hand there are always people who make it a point of honour to keep ahead of the game. Someone in the States has taken a leaf out of Archimedes' book. Remember he kept invading Roman ships at bay with large mirrors reflecting the sunlight? This guy has marketed a cheap laser pointer intended to blind CCTV cameras.'

'Times change,' said Monsieur Pamplemousse. 'Where will it all end?'

'That's only the beginning,' said Bonnard. 'Infiltrating people's computers via "silent deploy" – an unwanted email or a fake greeting card which unloads a program without having physical access – is getting to be old hat.

'It's now technically possible, using a laptop, to download information from mobile phones: lists of other people's phone numbers, their contacts, who they are meeting and when – all the information they thought was personal only to them.

'Wireless interconnectivity with computers is another way in through the back door; a window of opportunity, if you like. It is perfectly possible to read everything on someone's computer screen from a van parked a street away; all kinds of personal details, credit card numbers, you name it.'

'Is there no way of putting a brake on it?' asked Monsieur Pamplemousse.

'You can't stop people inventing things,' said Bonnard. 'It's what's known as progress. First of all you've got to find a manufacturer who admits his product is being used for illegal purposes. Once upon a time technology tried to keep up with people's needs. Now it's the other way round.

'Anyway, it isn't all bad. Take Echelon. It's an automated global system intercepting over three billion emails a day, looking for key words that might constitute a security threat. Then there are global positioning locators, police and home security networks, all looking after you and me.

'The down side is a lot of these things may seem relatively harmless by themselves, but add them all together…who knows what will happen when the software catches up and all this information gets to be pooled?

'Talking of things that are on record, I gather you want to see the film we made of last night's little how-do-you-do?'

Monsieur Pamplemousse had been starting to think he

would never get around to it. 'Want' wasn't quite the word he'd had in mind, but he could hardly say no at this stage.

Turning to face another bank of recorders, Bonnard pressed a button and Pommes Frites appeared on the screens, gathering speed as he raced down one of the corridors in hot pursuit of a Great Dane who was dragging a diminutive uniformed attendant behind him.

'Funny thing – we missed him arriving. But as soon as we picked him up going down a corridor all by himself we knew it meant trouble. It's one of the house rules; dogs must be accompanied at all times.'

'So you don't know where he came from?'

'No, more's the pity.'

Monsieur Pamplemousse offered up a silent prayer of thanks.

'It was a whirlwind chase, I can tell you. Given the fact that it was prime time for evening exercises, keeping up with it all was like a state-of-the-art computer game. That's when we switched to RECORD.'

Monsieur Pamplemousse found himself losing count of all Pommes Frites' encounters as he careered back and forth on the row of screens. Every sort of breed, from Afghan to Pekinese, seemed to be fleeing in all directions.

'It could be worse,' said Bonnard cheerfully. 'Think what it would be like if we had sound.'

'How many dogs are there staying in the hotel?'

'At a guess, about half as many as there were yesterday. Most of them checked out first thing this morning, taking their owners with them.'

'You don't have cameras in any of the rooms?' asked Monsieur Pamplemousse.

'If only…' Bonnard glanced back over his shoulder. 'I should be so lucky. I could take early retirement on the proceeds if we did! Ask any of the maids. The management would be pleased, too, that's for sure. Things disappear like magic; ashtrays, ice buckets, umbrellas, hairdryers…you name it. I swear some guests bring their own screwdrivers. It's a disease. Holiday Inn Hotels lose over 560,000 towels a year, and that's only a small part of it.

'Are you thinking of any room in particular?'

'Seven hundred and four,' said Monsieur Pamplemousse.

Bonnard looked at him over the top of his glasses. 'You've only picked our current number one item of interest. Funny couple.'

'Couple?'

'They checked in as Mr and Mrs Beardmore, but you never see them together. He eats in the hotel restaurant and she has all her meals sent up. We call her "*la Grosse Fromage*". That's all she has – every day of the week – cheese on toast. One of the commis chefs does nothing else but prepare them for her. Even then she doesn't always finish it.'

Something clicked in Monsieur Pamplemousse's brain. 'How long have they been here?'

'I can't tell you exactly. I can find out if you like.'

'Longer than a couple of nights?'

'They arrived over a week ago. And I'll tell you something else…'

Returning to the bank of video recorders, Bonnard pressed another switch. A picture came up showing an overhead view of the corridor outside Mrs Beardmore's room. Her door opened and a man came out, looked around furtively, then set off out of shot. He was picked up a moment later approaching the elevator.

Monsieur Pamplemousse eyed the screen thoughtfully. So Monsieur Leclercq's suspicions were correct after all.

'There is no reason why she shouldn't have a partner, of

course,' said Bonnard. She's paying for a suite. She can fill it with as many people as she likes within reason if that's what she wants to do. But it's odd that they never eat together.

'I'll show you what I mean.'

Reaching across the rows of buttons and faders he threw up a picture on another bank of monitors to the right of the main display. It showed a wide angle shot of the same man in a corner of the hotel restaurant. He looked vaguely familiar. Well-groomed, natty, seen on a black and white screen he had what Monsieur Pamplemousse's old mother would have called 'a touch of the tar brush'. But that had been long before the days of PC and she had never strayed far from the Auvergne where she had been born and brought up. Anyone from outside the region was an immediate object of suspicion.

'Is it possible to see a close-up shot of him?' asked Monsieur Pamplemousse.

'Unfortunately, no. The kitchen has control of the restaurant cameras. They have nothing to do with security. It's so that they can see how each table is progressing. It helps to keep the service running smoothly. We simply take a feed. I can tell you what he's eating though.

'*Feuillantine de Langoustine*. It's one of the chef's specials. He's had it three times already to my knowledge. *And* a bottle of Batard Montrachet to go with it. He doesn't stint himself.

'If it's important, I can use an electronic zoom, but it will lose definition. It's like a digital camera in that respect. Optical zooming enlarges the whole of the image on the sensor, with all the pixels intact. Electronic zooming simply takes a segment of the sensor and enlarges that, with the result that you end up filling the screen with correspondingly less pixels and definition suffers.'

'Don't worry,' said Monsieur Pamplemousse. It all sounded too complicated for his untrained mind.

As the pictures switched around the various tables in the restaurant he suddenly caught sight of another familiar figure.

'Can you hold it there?'

Bonnard pressed the still frame button. 'Someone you know?'

'The girl behind the group – eating by herself in a corner table.'

'The one in a white dress that leaves a lot to be desired showing?' Bonnard laughed. 'She's number two on the hotel's current popularity chart and coming up fast. We could build up a steady sideline selling blow-up pictures of her.'

Monsieur Pamplemousse was reminded of one of his colleagues, Truffert, and his stories of the days when he worked on a cruise ship. According to him, the officers used to keep a watchful eye on passengers as they embarked, singling out females who were travelling alone and placing bets on which one offered the best prospects.

'There's nothing like a long sea voyage for breaking down barriers,' was his favourite theme. Clearly hotels and ships had much in common.

'Is she staying in the hotel?'

'No, but she had *déjeuner* here the last two days. Always by herself.'

Monsieur Pamplemousse looked at his watch. It said 12.15.

'Is she booked in for today?'

'I'll find out for you.' Bonnard reached for a phone and cradled it under his chin. 'Get me the restaurant.

'Lunch isn't too difficult,' he said over his shoulder. 'Evenings are usually booked up weeks ahead. Even so, there are always a number of tables kept available until the last minute for residents. Besides, I think there will be a few more free from now on.'

He carried on a brief conversation into the mouthpiece.

'You're in luck's way,' he said.

'Could you book me in too?'

'Same table?'

'Please. I'd like it to be a surprise.' He waited while the other did the necessary.

'Done.' Replacing the handset, Bonnard turned and eyed Monsieur Pamplemousse curiously.

'It's none of my business, but if you get half a chance you might sound her out as to whether she would like a game of *pétanque*.

'As of today,' he said, registering Monsieur Pamplemousse's look of surprise, 'it's the start of "be extra nice to the customer week". No spitting in the pooches' dinner bowls when you think no one is watching. No helping them round corners with the toe of your boot. No saying they've been on a five-kilometre jaunt when they've only been halfway round the block and back. It's all on camera. Like so…'

Switching to yet another recorder, he threw up some behind-the-scenes examples.

Mindful of the hotel's icon in *Le Guide*, Monsieur Pamplemousse pretended he hadn't seen them. Monsieur Leclercq would be appalled if he knew the half of it.

'We're targeting the owners too. Indoctrinating them with freebie sessions aimed at introducing them to the French way of life – the Health and Fitness centre, cookery lessons, trips on the Seine – anything to smooth things over. Ten electrically powered Segways are being flown over from America. They've been rechristened Trottinettes and will be available for escorted tours. The official rate is seventy euros, but once again the hotel is doing it for free.'

'So where does *pétanque* come in?'

'That's another idea high on the agenda. We're trying to drum up custom. There are those among us who can't wait to see certain people bending over to pitch their boules in the Jardin du Luxembourg.

'I don't play the game myself, but I'm told that according to what is known as "The Fanny Legend", if a team fails to score a single point they are supposed to kneel and embrace the backside of a voluptuous female effigy that is kept for the purpose. I suspect our team will be hoping for the worst so that they can do it for real.'

Monsieur Pamplemousse couldn't help but think the members of the Association Sportif Jardin du Luxembourg might have something to say about that. They took the game seriously. Not only did they have mobile coat racks for use in the hot weather, but they kept their boules in numbered boxes behind a let-down flap in the side of their hut. They wouldn't take kindly to being invaded by a motley collection of outsiders from the Pommes d'Or. Speaking personally, for the time being he would stick to his usual haunt near the office.

'I owe you one,' he said, keeping those thoughts to himself. 'I'll see what I can do.'

'My pleasure,' said Bonnard. 'Besides, I had orders from on high to make sure you got all you wanted.'

'Good luck with your computers,' said Monsieur Pamplemousse as he took his leave. 'May their bugs be for ever little ones.'

'Computers are like Krispy Kremes,' said Bonnard, helping himself from the box. 'They're addictive. But at least Krispy Kremes are oven fresh. They do say the average computer mouse harbours four hundred times more bugs on its surface than any run-of-the-mill seat from a public toilet.'

'There's no answer to that,' said Monsieur Pamplemousse.

'Just don't sit on one, that's all,' said Bonnard. '*Bon appétit.*'

Trailing a couple of lengths behind the *Maître d'* as he steered a discreetly circuitous course around and between the tables and pillars of the Pommes d'Or's three Stock Pot restaurant, Monsieur Pamplemousse was acutely aware of two things. First of all, he was hardly dressed for the occasion, and secondly his movements were almost certainly being watched in various other parts of the hotel. He wouldn't have admitted it to anyone else but, despite the inaptitude of the analogy, his legs felt all fingers and thumbs, and he found difficulty in maintaining his normal easy gait.

It was ridiculous, of course. Covert surveillance had never bothered him in the past. But then, he had generally been on the other end of it. It was the first time he'd felt himself quite so much centre stage, as it were, caught in the full beam of the spotlight. The fact that the situation was entirely of his own making, and he had no idea where it was likely to lead him anyway, didn't help matters.

Even now, Bonnard was probably taking an anticipatory bite from one of his Krispy Kremes before pressing the RECORD button. Thank Heaven his enthusiastic espousal of the latest in security surveillance didn't embrace the addition of a sound track. That really would be inhibiting.

To be honest, he also missed having Pommes Frites at his side. It was like being bereft of his right arm.

Somewhere *en route*, between one pillar and the next, he registered the lone figure of the man who had already been pointed out to him on one of the Security Section's screens. It could have been a repeat performance of their feed from the kitchen.

Mrs Beardmore's husband, if that were indeed his station

in life – perhaps Toy Boy might be a better job description; seen in the flesh he looked younger than Claye, which wasn't difficult – was seated at exactly the same table near the far wall to his right. He was wearing a casual open-neck, light blue shirt beneath a single-breasted dark blue blazer.

It didn't need more than a cursory glance to confirm that he was tucking in to a *feuillantine de langoustine*. He felt the man's eyes following his progress across the room.

'Well! Look what the wind's blow in!' Glancing up from her menu as he drew near, Elsie registered genuine surprise.

'I am rapidly coming to the conclusion that the world is an even smaller place than it is said to be,' replied Monsieur Pamplemousse. 'I won't stop long, but do you mind if I join you for a moment or two?'

Taking advantage of the proffered chair, he made to sit down before she had a chance to answer; not that he expected her response to be anything other than welcoming.

'Would you care for a celebratory glass of champagne?'

''Ave you ever known me to say "No"?' asked Elsie.

Catching the *Maître d*'s eye, he gave a nod. In truth, it was a loaded question; impossible to answer without running the risk of causing offence, although once again he doubted if that would happen. Elsie was Elsie, and it wasn't in her nature to take offence.

During the brief moment the sliding of his chair into place afforded him, he did a quick mental replay of the last time he and Elsie had been together. As far as he could see, nothing had changed; the same deceptively innocent blue eyes returned his gaze, panning down and zooming in to a close-up of his own as he sat down. The effect was also very much as he remembered it. *Irrésistible!* There was no other word for it. Little things: the chemical reaction in the pit of his stomach as parts of it turned to water; a noticeable quickening of the pulse rate.

'Where's Pommes Frites got to, then?' said Elsie. 'Don't tell me they've put 'im inside after what went on last night.'

'You've heard about it?'

''Eard? I not only 'eard. I saw it. Went past me like a dose of salts 'e did. Didn't even stop to pass the time of day. Mind you, seeing the look in his eye I can't say I'm sorry.

'The last time we met, the first thing 'e did was stick his nose up you know where. Goodness knows what 'e would have done last night given 'alf a chance.'

'As I recall,' said Monsieur Pamplemousse, rising to Pommes Frites' defence, 'you were wearing a very short skirt at the time.'

'And 'e had a nose like a wet truffle,' said Elsie, not to be outdone.

'He was only trying to be friendly,' said Monsieur Pamplemousse lamely. 'He can't help himself.'

'That's what they all say,' replied Elsie. 'I've met 'is sort before.'

'*Pardon, Monsieur.*' The *Maître d'* handed him a menu before reluctantly taking his leave. Although clearly in an ideal world he would have been only too pleased to linger, perhaps making the most of enumerating various specialities of the day, his long years of training denied him the pleasure.

Not that Monsieur Pamplemousse would have blamed him. Elsie had that effect on most men. She was like a luscious peach, full of juice and ripe for plucking; a walking temptation for anyone passing to sink their teeth into the warm flesh. Although, that said, he strongly suspected that when it came down to it, as with her counterpart in the wild, she would be equally adept at keeping tantalisingly just out of reach.

While waiting for the champagne to arrive he made pretence of scanning the menu.

Not only was Elsie the stuff of which many men's dreams are made (and a good many women's too, if they could only bring themselves to admit it), she cooked like the proverbial angel. So much so, she could probably have told the chef a thing or two if she had a mind to.

They had first met when she was working as an English au pair to Monsieur and Madame Leclercq. One of her own specialities, until PC intervened and the powers that be insisted on renaming it, had been a dish called 'Spotted Dick'.

He rated it second only to her Yorkshire puddings, and his eulogising on such titbits of inside information at the staff get-together later that same year gave rise to a good many guffaws.

Unfortunately, human nature being what it is, the dice was heavily loaded against Elsie. Not content at having provided her with a pair of *doudounes*, the firmness and amplitude of which were far in excess of the national average, gilding the lily with more than a morsel of natural dexterity at the kitchen stove (a lethal combination in many men's eyes), mother nature had bestowed on her a generosity of spirit which manifested itself in a simple desire to share her good fortune with all those she came into contact with. It was an attribute that immediately aroused the suspicions of other members of her sex, the distaff side of married couples in particular. And whether or not they had just cause, who could blame them?

In vain had Monsieur Leclercq made much of what he swore were her perennial headaches. No one, least of all his wife, Chantal, actually believed a word of it. From the word go, the writing had been on the wall as far as Elsie was concerned. Her stay at the Leclercq's residence had been short and, it has to be said, a not entirely happy one.

Some while later, unbeknown to both Chantal and Doucette, for reasons best left unrecorded, and following a certain amount of behind-the-scenes pressure from Elsie herself, she had enjoyed a spell as the first and in all probability the last trainee female inspector working for *Le Guide*.

At the Director's bidding, it had fallen to Monsieur Pamplemousse to take her under his wing while he was working in the Bordeaux area. The vast sand dunes situated near Arcachon might well have told a tale or two on that score had the prevailing westerly gales not swept them clean at regular intervals during the succeeding winter months.

'Anyway,' said Elsie, breaking into his thoughts. 'Where did you spring from?'

'I was about to ask you the same question,' said Monsieur Pamplemousse.

She reached across the table and gave him a dig in the ribs. 'Couldn't keep away from you, could I? I'm only 'uman flesh and blood when all's said and done.'

Monsieur Pamplemousse began to feel doubly pleased the security system lacked sound.

Elsie reached under the table and withdrew a clipboard. 'Ron gave me this just before I came over. Don't tell anyone, but I'm 'ere on official business. I'm working as an 'ealth inspector for the French government, in I. All expenses paid.'

Monsieur Pamplemousse stared at her while the champagne arrived. It was the last thing he expected to hear.

'You? A health inspector?' he said, as soon as the waiter had gone.

Elsie tried to look hurt. Pursing her lips in a way that

could have cracked a light bulb at fifty paces, it had quite the opposite effect. 'What's wrong with that? You saying I'm un'ealthy or summock?'

'No, of course not. But…' Feeling hot under the collar, Monsieur Pamplemousse groped blindly for a passing straw. 'After all,' he said, 'you are not French…'

'Dear, oh dear,' said Elsie. 'Lose ten points and return to Go! That's not the end of the world, you know, even if you lot think it is. We're all in the Common Market now. Some of us is more in it than others, of course, but it's all a matter of flashing the right bit of paper and Ron saw to that. It's a work of art.'

Feeling for her handbag, she opened it and withdrew an official-looking document. 'Apart from a small matter of the ink being 'ardly dry, you can't tell it from the real thing…'ave a decko.'

Running his eyes over the piece of paper Elsie handed him, Monsieur Pamplemousse had to admit he couldn't fault it. Even the embossed heading looked genuine. But then, he didn't really know what to look for in the first place.

'It's like Ron says, so long as it looks kosher, who's going to query it?' said Elsie. 'Most people 'aven't seen the real thing anyway. Attach it to a clipboard like so…' she paused to demonstrate, 'and it'll get you anywhere.

'Anyway,' she raised her glass. 'Bottoms up! I've got my kit of parts and I'm all ready to go.'

Knowing she was almost bound to tell him, Monsieur Pamplemousse didn't even bother to ask what they were.

Instead, he watched while she moved a small vase of flowers from the centre of the table to one side. 'Close your eyes.'

Monsieur Pamplemousse did as he was told.

'Open them.'

Glancing down he saw that in place of the vase there was now a small transparent plastic box. He could have sworn something black inside it moved, almost as though blinded by the light.

'Meet Matilda,' said Elsie. 'Ron's pet cockroach. He says they 'aven't changed very much since Carboniferous times – that's over two hundred and fifty million years ago. Ron has time to study these things in the prison library. He says it's one of the best things about being inside.'

'Why are you telling me all this?' asked Monsieur Pamplemousse, dreading the answer and fearing the worst.

'Matilda's what you might call my insurance policy,' said Elsie.

'When Ron was working a scam as a catering adviser, 'e used to take 'er with him whenever 'e went out to eat in order to make sure 'e got good service.

'Mind you, 'e always played fair. 'E used to show Matilda to the owner first. "'Ow would it be," 'e used to say, all casual like, "'ow would it be if I found one of these in your soup doing the breaststroke? It wouldn't look too good, would it, 'owever beautifully it's been garnished? Especially if it gets to be shown on prime time television." Ron can be very persuasive when 'e likes.'

Monsieur Pamplemousse gazed in horror at the object in the box, then hastily moved his chair closer to the table in an effort to screen it from any cameras that might be trained in their direction. At least they were outside Bonnard's direct control, otherwise he would undoubtedly be zooming in for a tight close-up, probably choking on his Krispy Kremes in his excitement. Unfolding his own menu, he held it over the table for added protection.

'Put it away,' he hissed.

'What's the matter?' said Elsie innocently. 'A little cockroach won't do you no 'arm.

'Mind you, if you 'appen to be another cockroach and you're male it's a different matter on account of the fact that the female ones 'ave got funny habits; like if they're 'ungry they're not above eating the male even while they're 'aving it off. They start at the 'ead and work their way down. I expect they save the best bit until last. It must be a matter of timing really when they get near the end as to which 'as top priority. I keep telling Ron – 'e wants to watch out!'

Monsieur Pamplemousse was hardly listening. Visions of what might happen if Monsieur Leclercq got wind of what was going on flashed through his mind. And not simply the Director. The Media would have a field day if they picked up on the story. He could see the headlines. '*LE GUIDE* INSPECTOR INVOLVED IN RESTAURANT SCAM.' For a moment it felt as though his world was in danger of collapsing. He would never live it down.

'You can't do it,' he said. 'You *mustn't*. Promise me.'

Elsie gazed back it him with her big round blue eyes.

'Only if I 'ave to,' she said, noncommittally. 'My old grandfather always taught me – there's no such word in the English language as "can't".

'Besides, I don't know what Ron would do if 'e lost Matilda. 'E only taught 'er to swim didn't 'e? She's a lovely little mover. 'E made me promise on no account must I ever give 'er up. Show them your credentials, that's 'is motto. Say they can't 'ave 'er because she's scheduled to be exhibit "A" in any court case that comes up.' Reaching under the table, Elsie gave his left knee a squeeze.

'Don't worry. Like I say, it's an insurance policy. For use only in cases of emergency. We'd better make sure we don't 'ave one, that's all I can say.'

Withdrawing her hand, she took hold of his menu with the other. As she did so he realised the box had disappeared. 'It's a case of "Find the Lady" innit,' said Elsie, flashing him a warning signal with her eyes.

'My friend doesn't fancy the soup,' she announced, as a Head of Station waiter materialised, pad and pencil at the ready. 'Tell you what,' she continued, turning back to Monsieur Pamplemousse, 'why don't you 'ave some *Quenelles de brochet*? That's what I'm 'aving. Sure you won't change your mind and stay?'

'*Superb*!' said the waiter, nodding his approval.

Monsieur Pamplemousse felt himself weakening. It would be a grave dereliction of duty to visit a three Stock Pot restaurant and leave without tasting a single dish; one which would be hard to explain.

'Make that two,' he said.

'If I may also suggest, *Madame*…' leaning over Elsie's shoulder the waiter ran his pencil down the menu, indicating possible dishes to follow. It struck Monsieur Pamplemousse that while he was talking the man's eyes were not entirely directed where they should have been. He looked quite cross-eyed.

In response to a direct question, he held up his hand. 'I won't,' he said reluctantly. 'I shall have to go after the first course. Perhaps another time…'

'What's up?' asked Elsie, catching sight of Monsieur Pamplemousse smiling to himself after she had finished ordering. 'Is it summock I've said?'

He avoided the question. The truth was, he couldn't help being amused by the thought of trying to explain to anyone he knew that he'd been playing 'Find the Lady' involving a cockroach called Matilda. Especially if he let on whom he had been playing it with.

'Your extramural activities aside,' he persisted, 'what else are you up to?'

'Looking after Ron's interests,' said Elsie dodging the question. 'You know Ron. 'E's got 'is fingers in all sorts of pies.'

'Like funerals?' suggested Monsieur Pamplemousse, testing the water. 'If I am not mistaken, you were at Gaston's earlier in the week.'

'Me?' said Elsie. 'You want to take more water with it next time. Anyway, ask no questions, get told no lies. I was what you might call Ron's representative.'

'He knew Gaston?'

'In a manner of speaking,' said Elsie. 'Ron was very upset when 'e 'eard the news. He couldn't come 'isself on account of having 'ad his passport taken away from 'im, so I came instead.'

'So he is still in jail?'

'Yes,' said Elsie, 'and then again, no. He's not exactly out, like 'e's been released. He wouldn't be too keen on that anyway. The trouble was 'e kept getting 'is sentence reduced for good behaviour. Like I say, that'll teach 'im.'

Elsie paused as some *amuse-gueules* in the shape of small bowls of soup arrived at their table. Seeing the sommelier hovering nearby, Monsieur Pamplemousse shook his head briefly. If he wasn't careful he would find himself embroiled in a full-scale production number and he was anxious to report back to the Director.

'Anyway,' continued Elsie, 'one way or another Ron got fed up with the old place so 'e put in for a transfer. The thing is, they decided not to call it a jail any more in case it upset what they call the inmates and they needed counselling. That kind of thing costs money these days. It's now run by something called the National Offenders

Management Service.

'That was the last bleedin' straw as far as Ron was concerned. 'E got very up in arms about it. Reckons it's demeaning. 'E maintains the screws don't like it either on account of the fact that it upsets the delicate relationship they've built up and carefully nurtured over the years. They're thinking about coming out on strike. Well, the screws are thinking of coming out. The ones doing time will 'ave to stay in, of course. Not that it affects Ron any more…'

'You mean, he *is* out?'

'Not entirely,' said Elsie. ''E put in for a transfer to an open prison and it's come through.'

'An *open* prison?' repeated Monsieur Pamplemousse. As was so often the case with Ron's activities, he found difficulty in keeping up. 'You have such things? It sounds a contradiction in terms.'

'Not as far as Ron's concerned it ain't,' said Elsie. ''E makes full use of it. It suits 'im down to the ground. 'E's got all mod cons – television, fax machine, email on 'is computer, so most of 'is friends are on tap and at 'is beck and call. No aggro. Apart from all that, we see each other every other weekend to catch up on what 'e likes to call our "quality time" together. Ron 'as 'is needs like everyone else. 'E likes to give 'is what'sit an airing every now and then. Don't we all?'

Monsieur Pamplemousse forbore to answer the question. He had often suspected that Ron being almost permanently in jail suited both of them. Elsie always spoke warmly of their getting together on visiting days, and clearly he had his life extremely well organised and didn't really want for much.

'They allow such things?'

'I wouldn't like to be the warder what tried to stop 'im,' said Elsie. 'Accidents can 'appen. A lump of concrete falling off a roof can give a person a nasty 'eadache.'

Monsieur Pamplemousse began to wish he hadn't brought the subject up, but he was saved by the arrival of the first course.

It was all that Elsie said it would be. The oval shaped quenelles were beautifully firm, yet with a feather-light texture. He could picture them rising out of the water, breaking the surface like so many tiny whales when cooking was complete. A truly magical moment, but it needed a master's touch.

The filling was of finely ground pike. There was a hint of nutmeg, and the garnish was a basic sauce *Parisienne*, made with cream, eggs and butter, lightly seasoned with pepper and salt and a touch of lemon juice, to which sorrel had been added.

With it came a glass of delicious Le Soula Blanc Roussillon from Gérard Gauby. There was only one word to describe it: *Parfait*.

'You must allow me to pay for it.'

'In no way,' said Elsie. 'It's my treat – or rather, Ron's.'

She looked over her shoulder. ''E's in the money right now.'

'You still haven't told me why you are over here,' said Monsieur Pamplemousse.

Elsie pondered the problem for a moment. 'The thing is,' she said, 'Ron's done a deal with the French government in exchange for certain information. I'm over 'ere to collect the cash on account of the fact that it mustn't appear on the books…'

'You mean he is trying to avoid paying Income Tax?'

Elsie looked at him pityingly. 'Know any more jokes? It's what Ron calls "quid pro quo". Besides, 'e 'eld all the cards.'

'May I ask what sort of deal it is?' asked Monsieur Pamplemousse.

'You may ask,' said Elsie, 'but I can't tell you. It's all very 'ush 'ush. Like I told 'Enri…Ron says the fewer people who know about it the better.'

'Henri!' Monsieur Pamplemousse stared at her. 'You surely don't mean Monsieur Leclercq…'

'That's right. I put Ron in touch with 'im first of all because 'e knows so many people in what 'e likes to call the 'igher echelons.'

'But he told me it was an impeccable source.'

'Are you saying Ron can't be trusted?' demanded Elsie. ''E'd be most upset.'

'No, of course not, but…'

Reaching inside her bag again Elsie took out a mobile phone. 'The best thing you can do is speak to Ron 'isself about it.'

'He has a telephone too?'

''Course!' said Elsie, dialling a number. 'Ron couldn't live without 'is mobile. Always answers on the first ring.'

After a few seconds had passed she pressed the OFF button. ''E must be out shopping – either that or 'e's having a long lunch somewhere and doesn't want to be disturbed.'

'One day,' said Monsieur Pamplemousse, 'I must meet Ron.'

'Yeah, well,' said Elsie, darkly, 'I get the feeling that may be sooner than you think. In the meantime, I'll give you 'is number.'

Monsieur Pamplemousse took an old envelope from his wallet and handed it to her.

While Elsie was writing he had a sudden thought. 'I have to go, I'm afraid, but what would you say to a game of *pétanque*?'

'I've got to 'and it to you,' said Elsie, staring up at him. 'You don't give up, do you? I've never 'eard it called that before.'

'*Pétanque*,' said Monsieur Pamplemousse, 'is a form of boules. It is played in the open air – usually with lots of people watching.' Briefly, he passed on the news about the hotel's plans.

'Ah, well,' said Elsie, returning his envelope as he made to leave. 'That's life. One moment you're up, the next moment you're down. I've put my mobile number down as well in case you need me.'

'I will give you some lessons if you like.'

'Promises, promises,' said Elsie. '*Arrivederci!*'

'*Ciao*,' said Monsieur Pamplemousse.

It wasn't until he was on his way out that he noticed the man in blue was nowhere to be seen.

Emerging from the depths of the Da Vinci car park some half an hour or so later, he heard the familiar clink of metal balls making contact one with another to the right of the tarmac area. It was a satisfactory sound; the accompanying music to a game that was undoubtedly being played all over France at that very moment, and which needed no lyrics other than the occasional grunt.

The sound would have been slightly different in Roman times of course. In those days the boules had been fashioned out of stone. In between, artillerymen had played it with canon balls, doubtless producing an even deeper tone.

Having arrived at the Esplanade rather later in the day than was customary, there were more games than usual in progress. The coat hooks attached to one of the trees were full to overflowing.

The sun was still high in the sky and the various pitches

were laid out higgledy-piggledy in all directions as those whose turn it was to throw the tiny wooden *cochonet* opted as far as possible to make it land in one of the few shady areas still available.

Standing at the top of the steps, taking in the scene, Monsieur Pamplemousse became aware of a distant shape hurtling towards him from the direction of the Shanghai Chinese restaurant on the far side of the rue Fabert. A moment later Pommes Frites skidded to a halt at his feet, nearly knocking him over in the process.

For a moment or two it was all licks and ruffling of fur as master and hound were reunited; a case of absence making the heart grow fonder, if indeed that were possible. A casual bystander could well have been forgiven for thinking they had been apart for months rather than hours.

Talking of which…regaining his balance, he spotted a flash of colour not far away. It took him a moment or two to recognise the Director's secretary. He wasn't used to seeing Véronique in a flowery summer dress. It made a change from her usual black trouser suit. She must have gone straight into the office following his call. She waved as she drew near.

'Welcome back,' he said, holding out his hand.

'Thanks to you and Pommes Frites,' said Véronique simply. 'I was determined not to give in, and Monsieur Leclercq wasn't going to lose face.'

'No more handbag searches?'

'Not a word,' said Véronique. 'He did have the grace to explain to me what was going on. As if I didn't know! He tends to forget that a good secretary knows more about her boss than she is often given credit for.'

Monsieur Pamplemousse glanced down at Pommes Frites. Despite having had a good night's sleep, he was still looking slightly hung-over. Gazing round with his tongue hanging out, he was eyeing all the activity with interest. Joining in a game would do him the world of good.

'Would you mind waiting here while I fetch my boules from the car?' he enquired.

'At least one of us thought you would never ask,' said Véronique.

'And I've won my bet,' she said, when he returned. 'I told Monsieur Leclercq you wouldn't be able to resist a game before you got back.'

'You did? What did he say?'

'He was very pleased at the thought. He said he felt you had been overworking just lately – that and the heat. He was getting worried. Apparently, when you got back from the funeral you were rambling on about someone called Doctor Livingstone and a place called Ujiji. He couldn't find it anywhere on the map in his office.

'Anyway, I must get back. *Bonne chance.*'

Left to their own devices, Monsieur Pamplemousse moved into the open, a little away from the main crowd, and made ready to play. Having thrown the *cochonet* within the regulatory distance, he armed himself with the first of his four boules and threw it towards the jack. Much to his disgust, it landed wide of its target, but at least it would serve as a marker.

His second throw was invariably nearer, which proved to be the case on this occasion. Hopefully, the third throw would be better still. His best ever to date had ended up within two centimetres of its target, but that had been something of a fluke due to the stony ground.

He always allowed himself four throws. The first three in the role of the *pointeur*, aiming to place his boule as near to the jack as possible without actually touching it. For the remaining throw he became the *tireur,* the player who came in near the end and tried to knock the opponent's winning boule for six.

After which, it was Pommes Frites' turn to rush forward and collect the balls one by one. He enjoyed it so much, Monsieur Pamplemousse hadn't the heart to make use of his magnet on a string, although he was dying to have go with it.

Adopting a firm stance, knees bent, feet close together, he took hold of the fourth boule with his right hand in the prescribed manner; back uppermost, fingers together, and took careful aim, bending his wrist back in order to flick it forward when it was thrown.

Alongside him, he sensed Pommes Frites drawing himself up: muscles tensed, ears back, poised ready to spring into action the moment it had come to rest.

But before that, something totally unexpected happened.

There was a thud as another boule-like metal object landed halfway between them and the jack. It seemed to have come from the direction of the tree where all the coats were draped, effectively masking whoever was responsible.

Monsieur Pamplemousse could hardly believe his eyes. Not only was such a thing in direct contravention of Article 24, which clearly states that any boule whose trajectory caused it to land on someone else's territory should be declared null and void, but the object was in fact a good deal less than the regulation minimum diameter of 7.05 centimetres. Worse still, it had grooves cut into its surface! At first he thought it was someone's idea of a prank. Modifying a boule in any way whatsoever was a serious offence. If proven it could lead to a cancellation of a professional player's licence for a minimum of fifteen years.

These and other thoughts flashed through his mind at

lightning speed as Pommes Frites sprang into action, only to be erased in an instant as a cry of '*Couchez!*' rang out from somewhere near at hand.

All around him people froze. Such behaviour was beyond the pale. One of the rules of the game, Article 17 in fact, decreed that during a throw everyone had to remain quiet and refrain from walking about, gesticulating or doing anything that could distract the player's attention.

Pommes Frites, his instant reaction to sudden commands honed to razor-edged perfection over the years, literally hovered in mid-air for a fraction of a second, his feet going like paddles as another object flew past his head, missing it by a matter of millimetres.

Whoever had thrown the latest boule was obviously a *tireur* of some distinction, for it landed on the preceding object with the deadly accuracy of a guided missile, low down and a little to the right of centre, lifting it into the air and sending it flying upwards towards a tarmac area away from the crowd.

It was still gaining height when it exploded. Harmlessly, as it happened, but the shock silenced everyone around them and it was a moment or two before everybody began talking at once.

Hearing the pounding of feet coming from somewhere behind him, Monsieur Pamplemousse turned and was just in time to see a figure running across the Esplanade towards a waiting car. He was pursued by a second figure, already too far away to have any chance of catching up.

The first man was barely inside the back seat of what looked like a dark blue Renault Megane before it accelerated away, jumped the lights, and disappeared in an easterly direction towards the rue Saint Dominique. Given the distance and the angle, it was impossible to read the rear number plate.

Meanwhile, Pommes Frites, for the moment at least blissfully unaware of the narrowness of his escape from certain death, picked himself up from the spot where he had landed and looked round balefully for the person responsible.

Suddenly his expression changed. Jumping to his feet, his face lit up as he loped across the stony patch of ground to join his master.

'You realise, of course,' said Monsieur Pamplemousse, addressing the new arrival, 'that what you have just done is in direct contravention of Article 23, which states very clearly that any participant who plays a boule other than his own should receive a warning.'

'That may be true,' said Mr Pickering, 'On the other hand, in accordance with Article 4 of the *Fédération Française de Pétanque*, if a boule is broken into two or more pieces, the largest piece alone will count for measurement. Unfortunately, in this particular instance that is no longer possible. As far as I can see, there are no large pieces left.

'Perhaps,' he continued, bending down to exchange greetings with Pommes Frites, 'the time has come to rewrite the rule book. The possibility of someone substituting a hand grenade for a boule is clearly one the authorities haven't thought of. In the meantime, may I suggest we make ourselves scarce.'

Having ordered a *Cardinal* for Monsieur Pamplemousse and a *pastis* for himself, Mr Pickering left the bar and made his way towards a far corner of the room, away from the windows. 'By rights, Pommes Frites should be doing the honours,' said Monsieur Pamplemousse, moving his precious boules set to one side as his friend joined them. 'Or I ought to be doing it on his behalf. If you hadn't called out when you did, he wouldn't be here now.'

'I'll take a rain cheque.' Mr Pickering pulled up a chair. 'Anyway, if you want my opinion, it's a good thing we made ourselves scarce when we did. It saved us having to answer a lot of tedious questions.'

Monsieur Pamplemousse wasn't so sure. He'd heard the sound of police sirens coming from all directions while they were beating a hasty retreat along the rue Saint Dominique.

Admittedly, it had been in the opposite direction to the one the escaping car had taken, but once descriptions had been circulated it would be more a matter of putting off the evil moment. The police would lose no time in putting two and two together, particularly when they got to hear about the activities of a certain bloodhound, known to have already blotted his copybook once that week. It was for that very reason he'd suggested they find a quiet corner inside one of his regular haunts. Joining the crowd of sun-worshippers occupying the pavement tables outside would have been asking for trouble. At least it being the middle of the afternoon meant no one from *Le Guide*'s offices was likely to disturb them, but you never knew.

'I had no idea you were a *pétanque* player,' he said.

'It is one of my lesser-known accomplishments,' said Mr Pickering modestly. 'I must admit to being a little rusty, but for a short while I was the South of England champion.

'Once upon a time I had aspirations to become a trend-setter. *Pétanque* has a lot of things going for it. Apart from the fact that it can be played on any old patch of level ground, it has one thing in common with our own game of bowls: the players don't run around in ever decreasing circles shaking their fists in the air when they've scored a point. But I was fighting a losing battle. It doesn't attract the crowds. The world is becoming more violent by the day.

'All the same, I never thought I would live to see a hand grenade being thrown.'

'Things are worse in the south,' said Monsieur Pamplemousse gloomily. 'The mayor of Montpellier has had to cancel the annual *pétanque* tournament again this year. Since the arrival on the scene of Roma gypsies, the event has become open warfare. Knife-carrying spectators threaten players just as they are about to make a throw. Security dogs are the order of the day. Riot police are regularly called in. Things have become impossible.'

'No wonder you are so cool about what happened just now,' said Mr Pickering. 'It's small beer.'

Monsieur Pamplemousse shrugged. Inwardly he was feeling far from cool; his mind was in turmoil, wondering what would happen next. 'It is all to do with money. In Montpellier the winning team shares a cash prize of over seven thousand euros.'

'We live in strange times,' said Mr Pickering dryly. 'In England that would just about buy Beckham a new suit. Anyway, we must have a quiet game together when all this is over. As far as this afternoon's episode is concerned, I'm sure you would do the same for me should the need ever arise.'

And probably die in the attempt, thought Monsieur

Pamplemousse, under no illusions as to his prowess.

'When…' he said. 'In the meantime, I had better get some practice in.'

'Don't worry,' said Mr Pickering. 'I doubt if I could give a repeat performance in a million years.'

'Don't tell me it was luck…'

'Not entirely,' said Mr Pickering. 'It is what is euphemistically known as "rising to the occasion". At such times it needs more than luck. You might say a professional golfer is lucky when he drives off and gets a hole in one, but since that is precisely what he is aiming to do, it would hardly be fair.

'I think it has more to do with the coming together of all manner of forces in a moment of intense concentration.'

They both fell silent as the *madame* arrived with their order. Having wiped the table-top clean and arranged coasters and glasses to her liking, she placed a bowl of water on the floor.

'*Comme d'habitude,*' she said. Pommes Frites lapped at it gratefully before settling down to think matters over. He was used to things like exploding fire-crackers – they had been part and parcel of the training during his early days with the Paris *Sûreté*, but it was the first time he had ever encountered an exploding boule. It seemed to him that if whoever threw it had been aiming for his master, he wasn't a very good shot. That he himself might have been the intended target hadn't yet crossed his mind.

'I'm afraid it may have put him off picking up boules for a while,' said Mr Pickering, intercepting the thought-waves emanating from under the table. He glanced up as Monsieur Pamplemousse took a sip from his glass. 'Good?'

'It is always good here,' said Monsieur Pamplemousse. 'The *Crème de Cassis de Dijon* is from Edmond Briottet and is high in alcohol. Also, it is made with just the right ratio of chilled Beaujolais. *Madame* knows how I like it, but today it is probably the best *Cardinal* I have ever tasted. Why? Because it might well have been my last.'

He watched as Mr Pickering slowly and carefully added some cold water to his glass.

'You will find the *pastis* is of the same high quality. It is from Henri Bardouin, and is full of complex flavours and the smell of wild herbs from the Lure Mountain. One glass is usually more than sufficient.'

'That is good,' said Mr Pickering, 'because I also feel in need of something strong. As Shakespeare would have it, "methinks there is something rotten in the state of Denmark".'

He concentrated his gaze on the liquid in the bottom of his glass as it clouded over, its milky whiteness momentarily assuming the classic wraith-like figure. 'Perhaps it's a good thing I didn't live in the days when absinthe was all the rage. At times like this I might easily have become addicted to the hallucinogenic qualities of wormwood; the whole ritual of it, in fact. The slow adding of the water to the sugar lump resting in its metal bridge.

'What was it Oscar Wilde said? "The first glass enabled him to see things as he wished they were; wonderful, curious things", and the second made him see things as they are not.'

'If I remember rightly,' said Monsieur Pamplemousse, 'didn't he also say of the third glass, "It makes you see things as they really are, and that is the most horrible thing in the world"? It drove him mad in the end, along with Verlaine, Toulouse-Lautrec and many others before it was outlawed.'

'You are right,' sighed Mr Pickering. 'I've probably had a lucky escape. I was simply trying to get a feel of what is going on. It seems to me the world is not as happy a place as it ought to be. It is in a constant state of flux. People are no longer happy with their lot.

'What would you say is the average Frenchman's pipe dream?'

'In the Auvergne,' said Monsieur Pamplemousse, 'where I was born, they used to dream of moving to Paris and opening a bar or a small restaurant. But that doesn't seem to be the case any more. Nowadays it is the other way round.'

'In England,' said Mr Pickering, 'for many people the dream used to be a thatched cottage in the country with roses round the door and two point four children, but I doubt if that is so any more. There have been too many disappointments over the years.

'These days they are more likely to end up in the Loire Valley, restoring some old barn, having first made sure the nearest village shop stocks Oxo cubes, Tetley teabags and Bird's custard. English people like the idea of France, but in trying to make it more like home they end up destroying the very things they came away to find.'

'The last time I saw you,' said Monsieur Pamplemousse, 'I thought you were heading back to England.'

'The last time you saw me,' said Mr Pickering, 'I thought so too. Before I reached Calais I had a change of mind. Or rather, my mind was changed for me.

'Word reached me that things were beginning to move. I gather there has been a major development. A demand for a large sum of money has been made; the equivalent of some ten million English pounds. Currently the French government is awaiting instructions.'

'Do they know where it came from?' asked Monsieur Pamplemousse. 'Or, more importantly, from whom?' He wondered if the AZF were up to their tricks again. It bore the same hallmarks; first the threat, then the demand, followed by a series of bizarre instructions, such as having the money placed on top of a tall building so that it could be collected by a helicopter.

'I was hoping you would tell me,' said Mr Pickering. 'Strictly speaking, since the threat is aimed directly at France, I only have a watching brief on behalf of my own government, but I gather you are involved in some kind of emergency "think tank".'

'Not so much a "tank",' said Monsieur Pamplemousse, 'more a small bowl.'

It would have sounded rather lame to say that, apart from Monsieur Leclercq, the only other person he had met was Mrs Beardmore, but it was early days and events had moved so quickly it was hardly surprising. He guessed the Director must be in touch with others.

'Mostly we are concerned with the "how" rather than "who" or "why".'

'It may prove hard to separate them,' reflected Mr Pickering. 'It could be a chicken and egg situation. Forgive the analogy with food, but if you want to find out what makes a particular egg taste the way it does, the first thing you do is find out what the chicken has been eating.'

Monsieur Pamplemousse gave a noncommittal shrug. It was all too easy to become paranoid about the whole thing. The mere mention of the word 'egg' immediately set his mind wondering whether or not they could be a possible target for a terrorist attack.

And yet…and yet… He still couldn't rid himself of Mrs Beardmore's notion that it might coincide with some kind of seasonal event…something that was a cause for celebration. A national holiday, perhaps…or the arrival from the Landes of the first white asparagus in May.

He launched yet another balloon in the air.

'If it were *aspèrge*,' he said, 'then ideally it needs to be eaten the day it is picked, so there is always a rush for it. Being grown so far away creates a problem. Sometimes it can be over a day old…

'*Alors!*' He threw up his hands. 'But it could be injected with something *en route* rather than at source…'

Mr Pickering gave sigh. '*Alors*, indeed! What it is to have such problems. I envy you your vast resources. If you wanted to inject asparagus at source in the UK, you would stand a better chance doing it seven thousand miles away in Peru, which is where most of it comes from.

'For the vast majority of English people, "fresh" means it was fresh when it was picked on the other side of the world. We used to be a nation of small shopkeepers and farmers, but sadly that is no longer the case. We have slowly found ourselves at the mercy of a few giant supermarkets that call the tune.

'France has them too, but at the same time you are very protective of your way of life. You still manage to retain your small shops and, being largely self-supporting agriculturally, you are rich in possibilities. It could be so many things.'

Mindful of the Director's warnings, and without naming names, Monsieur Pamplemousse enlarged on his meeting with Mrs Beardmore. Stripped of all its undercurrents, which in the light of day he had to admit might sound like something out of a cheap novelette, it didn't add up to much.

'It was rather one-sided,' he said, 'I have a feeling she had been hoping to get more out of me than I was able to supply.'

'I am not in the habit of surfing the web,' said Mr Pickering, 'but I take it this cookery guru is American?'

'Very,' said Monsieur Pamplemousse. 'CIA. Specially flown over for the occasion.'

'Then frankly, I am not surprised. She is probably coming up for air. US security is currently in danger of sinking under the weight of information flooding in from all over the world.

'Some of it is true, much of it is false. The problem lies in sorting out the wheat from the chaff. At the moment they have a monumental storage problem.

'Prior to 9/11, the CIA relied on an Information Retrieval system that could only translate text written in the Roman alphabet. With over six thousand languages in the world, that's only skimming the surface. Until they have the new multi-lingual National Virtual Translation Centre in Washington up and running it's likely to remain that way. When everything is in place there will be a few early retirements on both sides of the Atlantic.

'Even then, the machine has yet to be built that can understand and evaluate the subtle nuances in the way people write. Many words defy translation. It isn't just a matter of literal translation, it needs careful analysis too; interpreters to interpret the interpreters. And as if all that isn't enough, there are a dozen or more different branches of security after the same information for different reasons. Sharing that information doesn't always happen as it should.'

Mr Pickering paused for a moment to allow the size of the problem to sink in. 'Did your contact have any idea where the warning originated?'

'We didn't get around to discussing that,' said Monsieur Pamplemousse.

'It is all a question of communication,' said Mr Pickering. 'Most of the time there is too little, but there are occasions when you can have too much. It is a matter of striking the right balance.

'Apart from the traffic provided by their own agents using normal methods of coded communication, the CIA receives information by the truckload from outside sources, in every language under the sun and in every shape or form you can possibly imagine – from grubby scraps of paper bearing a cryptic warning in Arabic passed on in some remote Afghanistan bazaar, to waterlogged notebooks recovered from sunken boats that defy even the most sophisticated character recognition software.

'Not that we're entirely immune on our side of the Atlantic,' he continued. 'It was largely one such scrap of information that led me to attend Gaston's funeral.'

'I had wondered,' said Monsieur Pamplemousse.

'I am so sorry,' said Mr Pickering. 'If I had known about your own involvement in the current problem I would have come clean at the time, particularly as it was through you – something you had said to Gaston some time or another – that made him get in touch with me in the first place.

'A few weeks before he died he contacted me saying he needed some information to do with the British end of a trail he was following up. I wasn't able to help as it happened. But the encounter stayed in my mind.'

'On the subject of unexpected sources...' began Monsieur Pamplemousse. It was an abrupt change of subject, but it had been brought about by something Mr Pickering had said earlier. His mention of Bird's custard reminded him of Elsie. He had no idea what she did to it, but whatever it was, when used as an accompaniment to her Spotted Dick, it raised the dish to new heights.

'Someone called Ron has been talking to the French government. It may have nothing to do with what Gaston was after, but on the other hand…'

'Say that again,' said Mr Pickering. 'The name rings a bell.'

Monsieur Pamplemousse took the opportunity to bring him up to date on his lunchtime meeting.

'Interesting.' Mr Pickering added more water to his glass. 'Do I detect a common thread; the coming together of a number of disparate strands? You think this Ron is a reliable source?'

'For what it is worth,' said Monsieur Pamplemousse, 'my government clearly thinks so, and I must say that over the years I have come to the conclusion there are few better. He enjoys certain advantages denied to the rest of us. And I would say woe betide anyone who tried to lead him up the garden path.'

'But he didn't have any ideas on what form the attack would take?'

'If he did, Elsie wasn't free to talk about them.'

'In that case we shall probably never know,' said Mr Pickering. 'With great respect, your Intelligence people are past masters in the art of wheeling and dealing.

'Something is afoot. When I tried to sound them out they shut up like a clam. They were very nice about it, of course. Nice, but remarkably unforthcoming. One of them even went so far as to paraphrase a weather forecast I had read that very morning in *Le Parisien*: "Monsieur Celsius, having been lying dormant for a while, is showing signs of restiveness. Don't worry if some large cumulus clouds pass over your head. They will be disarmed and are simply in transit prior to being vaporised."

'Snooty bugger. I was left not knowing whether to carry an umbrella when I went out, or go shopping for a bullet-proof vest.'

'He was probably a product of one of the elite Grandes

Écoles,' said Monsieur Pamplemousse. 'Humility is not one of their required subjects.

'The American did come up with one suggestion,' he added, feeling he ought to redress the balance of information in some way. 'She wondered about the possibility of whoever is behind the current threat injecting truffles with poison. She pointed out that doing that would concentrate any attack on what she called "the movers and shakers" of our society.'

'Even more interesting,' said Mr Pickering thoughtfully. 'That doesn't sound like Al-Qaeda thinking. On the whole they tend to go for spectacular targets; almost at random you might say, yet clearly thought out, which is both good and bad. It is hard to predict where they will strike next; harder still to combat fanatics who are prepared to commit suicide in support of their cause.

'Poisoned truffles? It might well work in France, where they are greatly prized. Lots of countries wouldn't recognise a truffle if they saw one, and if they did they would probably leave it on the side of their plate.'

'If it *were* the case,' broke in Monsieur Pamplemousse, 'we haven't all that long to go. It is currently exercising the mind of my Director to the exclusion of all else. Mostly, I fear, for selfish reasons.'

'It wouldn't be easy,' mused Mr Pickering. 'They are hardly plentiful at the best of times, and this year, after all the heat, they will be practically worth their weight in gold. That being the case, they will be even more closely guarded than usual by those who make a living sniffing them out. Secrecy is the name of the game. The sheer ergonomics of injecting as many as possible of them with poison at the same time is hard to picture, so the fall-out might not be as great as one would think.

'A banquet for a visiting head of state, perhaps? The American President, for example. That would have undreamed of repercussions all over the world.'

Monsieur Pamplemousse fell silent. Such a catastrophic event didn't bear thinking about.

'You have a faraway look in your eyes, Aristide.'

'By a strange coincidence, where we are now is only a stone's throw from the rue Surcouf where Doucette and I were eating out on the night of the storm.'

'You think things are going the full circle?'

'I have a feeling they are heading that way,' said Monsieur Pamplemousse. 'They have to end somewhere. It's a kind of closing in.'

'Strange the attack on Pommes Frites should happen so near your office,' said Mr Pickering. 'It's almost as though someone is second-guessing your movements. There's no possibility of a leak anywhere?'

Monsieur Pamplemousse shook his head. 'Monsieur Leclercq's secretary is the only other person in the know, and I would stake my life on her discretion.'

Mr Pickering slowly drained his glass while he considered the matter.

'This morning,' he said, 'I passed a building site – a shop which had been gutted and was in the process of being transformed by two workmen into an establishment selling mobile phones, or so the notice outside proclaimed.

'They had constructed an arrangement of paint tins and planks to form a table, which they had then covered with a spotlessly clean white cloth. On top of that they had laid two place settings; china plates and the appropriate cutlery and glasses for the wine. They were about to partake of what to me seemed like a passing good selection of various meats and bowls of salad ingredients. The wine was a Brouilly from Duboeuf. I wish now I'd had a camera with me.'

'Why are you telling me this?' asked Monsieur Pamplemousse.

'Because,' said Mr Pickering, 'I don't think it would have happened anywhere else in the world. It was as French in its way as Cartier-Bresson's picture of the family having a picnic on the banks of the Seine, or the one he took of people strolling in the grounds at Glyndebourne, which had England written all over it.'

'*C'est normale*,' said Monsieur Pamplemousse. 'He was a past master at that kind of thing. The exact moment that says it all. Besides, food is an important part of French life.'

'The interesting thing about it,' continued Mr Pickering, 'is that in all three cases passers-by wouldn't have given such scenes a second glance. Being French, they certainly didn't stop to watch my builders tucking in to their lunch. At Glyndebourne they probably looked the other way so as not to be considered rude.'

'People tend to act the way they are brought up,' said Monsieur Pamplemousse. 'These things are deeply ingrained. What passes for normal in one country is looked on as being totally bizarre in another.'

'Precisely. The very point I am trying to make. By the same token, when it comes to getting rid of a dog, I don't think it would enter the head of the average Frenchman, or an Englishman come to that, to use a hand grenade in the hope that he would pick it up and blow himself to Kingdom Come. Poison perhaps, or in an extreme case a bullet from a gun after dark, but not a grenade in full daylight.

'By the same token I think one can rule out terrorism in the accepted meaning of the word.

'My feeling, for what it's worth, is that whoever was responsible for both that and the blowing up of the coffin wanted to make a statement in the clearest possible manner.

'It also strikes me that you must have been under surveillance for rather more than a few days for them to know about your interest in *pétanque* and the fact that Pommes Frites had a habit of joining in. Also, whoever was responsible didn't just happen to be passing by.

'The whole thing leaves a distinctly unpleasant taste. Much as one abhors terrorism in any shape or form, at least the followers of Al-Qaeda are fighting for something they believe in. Blackmailers are a particularly despicable form of life. Get rich quick at any price. Coercion at its very worst. In this case it is big money they are after, and from the style of their thinking, if push comes to shove, the loss of human life is a minor consideration.'

Glancing at his watch as it emitted a bleep, he made a face, then signalled for the bill. 'I have to leave you, I fear.

'We will keep in touch. In the meantime, don't forget Rusik.'

'Rusik?' Monsieur Pamplemousse had to think for a moment.

'Rusik and Pommes Frites have, or *had*…a lot in common. Rusik knew something his master didn't, but he was unable to communicate what it was. Consequently, he suffered the ultimate penalty in a manner calculated to show both contempt for those in authority and at the same time serve as a warning to others.

'It is still my belief that Pommes Frites knows something. He may not even be aware of what it is himself at the moment, but someone is out to get him and he is not exactly hard to spot.'

Mr Pickering held out his hand. 'I suggest it is perhaps wise if we are not seen together just at this moment. People might put two and two together and make rather more than four.'

It struck Monsieur Pamplemousse as being an eminently sensible suggestion. In the circumstances, following a set routine had been a cardinal error and he ought to have known better. Having given it a few minutes, he made his way back along the rue Saint Dominique. Pausing at the point where it joined the rue Fabert, he peered cautiously round the corner. The boules area had now been cordoned off by yellow incident tape, but the crowds had dispersed, along with the players, and, as far as he could see, so, for the time being at least, had the police.

Taking the bull by the horns, he signalled Pommes Frites to stay close to his side and together they made their way towards the pedestrian entrance of the car park. Having located his car, he got down on his knees and felt along the underside of the bodywork.

Almost immediately he made contact with a small plastic box. It was held in place by means of a magnet; one tug and it came away in his hand. He held it up to the light. Not much bigger than the size of a cigarette pack, it was clearly a battery operated transponder; in other words, the transmitting end of a Global Positioning System. He wondered how long his 2CV had been appearing as a moving dot on someone's PC screen. The device certainly hadn't been in place before the storm; he'd given the car a thorough going over shortly afterwards. Nor had he noticed anything untoward when he'd given it another clean before setting off for the funeral.

Mr Pickering was right. Someone, somewhere, must be sufficiently interested in his movements to have gone to the trouble of installing the device. It was yet more food for thought. Slipping the object into his jacket pocket, he packed the boules set under the front seat and led the way back up the stairs and out onto the esplanade.

Heading in the direction of *Le Guide*'s headquarters and catching sight of the familiar green of a *moto-crotte* street cleaner approaching, he paused for a moment before mounting the pavement on the far side of the rue Falbert.

Having spotted the man at the controls cast a suspicious glance in Pommes Frites' direction, it was a case of better safe than sorry. As a body, operators of the machines with their mobile vacuum hoses were not noted for being over-zealous in their regard for canine susceptibilities at the best of times, and it was probably his last sortie of the day.

Taking advantage of the momentary diversion as man and machine went past, he removed the transponder from his pocket and placed it on the rear mud shield. The operation took less than a second, and the notion that before the end of the day the device would literally end up in the *merde* struck him as being an eminently satisfactory solution to the problem.

Chapter Eight

'Thank goodness you are both safe, Aristide.' Monsieur Leclercq came forward to greet Monsieur Pamplemousse and Pommes Frites as they entered the Holy of Holies.

'When I first heard the bang I assumed it was a car backfiring. Even after Rambaud reported there had been an attempted assassination somewhere nearby I didn't put two and two together.

'It was Véronique who insisted we look into the matter, so I sent her out to reconnoitre the ground. It wasn't until she returned with the news that the boules area had been cordoned off and you were both missing that I began to fear the worst.'

'I am sorry if you were alarmed unnecessarily,' said Monsieur Pamplemousse. 'We were taking refuge in a nearby café.'

'Very wise,' said the Director.

He crossed to the windows and peered through one of the slatted blinds. 'It is getting a little too close for comfort, Pamplemousse. First the blowing up of the coffin, now this. What kind of world are we living in where these things can happen?'

Monsieur Pamplemousse exchanged glances with Véronique. 'Luckily, *Monsieur*, your office is on the top floor.'

It was like water off a duck's back. Monsieur Leclercq obviously agreed with him wholeheartedly.

'Presumably it is the same evil hand at work,' he continued, returning to his desk. 'That being the case, Aristide, I suggest you take the utmost care in future. We can ill afford to lose your services at this juncture, but I see you have some leave due…'

'*Merci, Monsieur*,' said Monsieur Pamplemousse. 'However, it wasn't me they were after.'

'What!' The Director stared at him. 'Then who?' He glanced down at Pommes Frites. 'You don't mean…'

'If it hadn't been for the prompt action of a very good friend of mine he wouldn't be here now.'

As succinctly as possible, he explained what had happened.

'This is terrible, Aristide,' said Monsieur Leclercq, when he had finished. 'But why are they after Pommes Frites? It surely can't simply be an act of revenge for his part in forestalling what might have been a massacre at the crematorium? If that were the case, to put it bluntly, why go to such bizarre lengths? Why not simply use a gun and have it over and done with?'

'I suspect the answer to the first question,' said Monsieur Pamplemousse, 'is that, like it or not, he is in possession of some vital piece of information which, for the moment at least, he is unable to pass on. He may not even realise the importance of it himself – time alone will tell.

'As for their using a gun, the person who was responsible for saving his life put his finger on it. Explosive devices serve a dual purpose; they eliminate the problem whilst at the same time achieving the maximum amount of publicity. Think what a field day the media would have had in both cases had they been successful.'

Véronique gave a shudder. 'It doesn't bear thinking about.'

'If only he could talk,' said Monsieur Leclercq.

His expression softened as he gazed across the room at Pommes Frites, on the one hand guarding the water bowl in case it got taken away again, on the other, having heard his name being bandied about, doing his best to follow the course of the conversation, looking from one to the other as they spoke.

'He is able to communicate most things very clearly when he wants to,' said Monsieur Pamplemousse, loyally, 'but there are times when he plays his cards close to his chest.'

'One thing is certain, Aristide,' said Monsieur Leclercq. 'From now on he must keep a low profile. I shall never forgive myself if anything happens to him. As I have said before, I feel it is all my fault he became involved in the first place.'

'Keeping a low profile isn't what bloodhounds are best at,' said Monsieur Pamplemousse. 'They make large targets and they are not used to hiding away.'

'Have you ever considered some form of disguise?' asked the Director. 'I was thinking about it only last night. Cosmetic surgeons can work wonders these days. My wife knows a very good man. I'm sure he could do something about his jowls, for example. A few tucks here and there would alter his appearance out of all recognition. At the same time we could arrange for a top artist in the field of make-up to raise his eyebrows and perhaps have his fur dyed, along with certain other embellishments. I would be more than happy to take Madame Grante into my confidence and make sure no expense is spared. I know she will agree if I explain matters to her. Deep down, she has a soft spot for dogs and we have a special fund for exceptional matters.'

'It is very kind of you,' said Monsieur Pamplemousse. 'But what is done cannot always be undone. A bloodhound's jowls are there for a purpose; they help concentrate their mind on the scent. Without that faculty they are lost. I wouldn't want to see him having to walk around for the rest of his life wearing a fixed smile on his face to no good purpose.'

'How about equipping him with some kind of body armour?' suggested Monsieur Leclercq. 'I have in mind the sort the American President clearly wears. The poor man is only able to walk in a straight line. You can see that whenever he appears on television. One of these days they will point him in the wrong direction and he will disappear over the horizon.'

'In Pommes Frites' case that would be worse than putting him into a strait jacket,' said Monsieur Pamplemousse. 'In any case it would only result in drawing even more attention to him.

'As it is, I hesitate to take him home with me for fear of putting my wife at risk. Doucette has no idea what is going on, and I would rather leave it that way for the time being.'

'He could stay with me,' broke in Véronique. 'It won't be what he is used to, but I would love to have him.'

'Certainly not!' said Monsieur Leclercq. 'I forbid you to put your own life in jeopardy. Besides, I need your presence in the office. He can stay here with me for the time being.

'I have decided to make the office flat my headquarters,' he explained. 'I am being pressed for an early update on our findings and apart from the fact that I cannot afford to lose time travelling to and fro, the last part of the journey is very deserted late at night. I wouldn't wish my wife to be worried.'

Monsieur Pamplemousse considered the pros and cons of the suggestion and ended up with the scales heavily weighed against it. Monsieur Leclercq had to be stopped at all costs.

'What a splendid idea, *Monsieur*,' he said. 'I am sure you will soon get used to the amount of work involved. A big plus will be taking him for a walk in the mornings. Twice round the Esplanade should be ample. There is no need to do it more than once in the evening. He likes having plenty of time for his dinner. It shouldn't be too large, otherwise he is inclined to snore, but I can give *Monsieur* a list of his favourite dishes and how he likes them cooked.

'Then there is the small matter of rubbing his nose with Vaseline every night before he goes to bed. Bloodhounds suffer from dry nose syndrome. It upsets their sense of smell, and I'm sure you will agree it is especially important to keep Pommes Frites' in good working order at the moment. It has been particularly bad this year with all the hot weather we have been having.

'I would suggest, *Monsieur*, that in any case you don't go out too late at night. Whoever was responsible for the latest attempt on his life is clearly conversant with our daily routine, and if they see me leaving without him they will put two and two together. I'm not sure how many others remain in the building overnight at this time of the year, but rest assured, Pommes Frites is a light sleeper and he almost always wakes at the first creak. If he shares your bed, as I am sure he will want to, there will be no cause for alarm…'

'May I make a suggestion, *Monsieur*?' Reading the signs on her boss's face, Véronique broke into the conversation. 'How would it be if you stay in a hotel for the time being? We could find one which welcomes dogs. Not the Pommes d'Or, of course, but there are others…

'As it happens, only the other day I began preparing a list of suitable establishments to go with our new symbol…'

As she hurried out of the room to fetch her notes Monsieur Pamplemousse sought to keep the idea afloat before the Director went cold on the suggestion.

'How about L'Hôtel?' he suggested, reminded of it by his conversation with Mr Pickering. 'It has the merit of being tucked away in the rue des Beaux-Arts. It is also very cosmopolitan and it caters for the rich and famous. As *Monsieur* will be aware, things have changed a good deal since Oscar Wilde stayed there. They do say it is even possible to sleep in the very bed he once occupied, complaining to the last about the wall-paper and the fact that he was "dying beyond his means".'

'Hardly an attractive thought, Pamplemousse,' boomed the Director. 'He said a lot of things in his time, but I doubt if he mentioned the size of the rooms there. I am told they are mostly too small to swing a kitten let alone a mature bloodhound.'

Much to Monsieur Pamplemousse's relief, Véronique reappeared at that moment brandishing a handful of brochures.

'It's a pity you won't be travelling in on Virgin Atlantic,' she said. 'Pommes Frites would qualify for a "Flying Paw" reward, entitling him to a T-shirt and a sparkling tag. On the other hand, with British Airways he would have to check in as excess baggage…' She glanced across the room. 'That wouldn't come cheap!

'There is an even bigger choice of hotels than I thought,' she added hastily.

'"Given advance notice, any dog currently taking up residence at the George V can have its name embroidered on the bed cover"…that doesn't sound like Pommes Frites.

'Then there's the Crillon… "The Crillon welcomes canine guests with a specially engraved collar tag, along with a designer sleeping basket containing a buffalo-hide bone, a bottle of its favourite mineral water, and the services of a bi-lingual vet… The daily menu includes thinly sliced breast of chicken…"

'Failing that, if you were to stay at the Trianon Palace, they offer a package deal where a dog can share a de luxe double room with its owner and enjoy round the clock room service. Poached hambone with vegetables is on the menu, followed by yoghurt. And they are given a miniature bottle of "Oh My Dog!" perfume when they leave.

'On the other hand, there is the Meurice. They allow clients to hold dog parties in their Belle Etoile suite…'

Véronique's voice trailed away as Monsieur Leclercq suppressed a shudder. Obviously, he was rapidly going off the boil.

'Embroidered bedspreads,' he snorted. 'Name tags; round the clock service; parties…all these things negate the whole object of the exercise. What happened to *anonymat*? *Anonymat* is the key word. Unless we can preserve anonymity the whole operation is off.'

Véronique hesitated. 'There *is* one other,' she said doubtfully, detaching a sheet of plain paper from the rest. 'I know you will say I'm what the Americans call "reference book impaired", but I came across it while I was surfing the web. It is listed under Hotdogholidays.com.

'I'm afraid it isn't very central. In fact, it is on the outer edge of the 16th *arrondissement*; very close to the Bois de Boulogne…'

'It might as well be in the middle of Outer Mongolia,' said the Director gloomily.

'I felt *Monsieur* might find it a little, how shall I say?…not up to your usual standards,' said Véronique. 'However, it is particularly recommended by the Kennel Club of America. They list "dog training" and "conversational aids", whatever they might be, under extramural activities. If it is a case of being anonymous I doubt if you will find anyone there you know, or vice versa…'

Good girl, thought Monsieur Pamplemousse. You've got the message. Game, set and match!

It was now or never.

'If I might also make a suggestion, *Monsieur*,' he said. 'Véronique has given me an idea. What better way would there be of preserving your anonymity, and that of *Le Guide's* too, if you were to check in, not as a Frenchman, but as one of our friends from across the Atlantic?'

'You mean…an American?'

Steady, thought Monsieur Pamplemousse. One idea at a time.

He waited while Monsieur Leclercq registered first of all surprise, then wonder, followed by signs of his interest having been aroused.

'Your command of the latest American buzz words is, if I may say so, *Monsieur*, legendary. Then again, I vividly recall the piece you once wrote for the staff magazine telling of your early thespian activities when you were still at school. It couldn't have been easy taking on the part of Robespierre at the tender age of thirteen. Given your background, playing the part of a man who led such a frugal life can hardly be called type casting. I dearly wish I had been there to see it, although you made the whole thing come alive for *L'Escargot's* readers.

'Take Robespierre's skilful oratory whenever he addressed the National Assembly… How many times was it? Five hundred? To have put that across without producing severe *longueurs* can have been no easy task. Then again, his passionate fight for liberty which made so many people in high office his enemy, not to mention his unremitting attacks on the privileged classes, must have required great acting ability for one such as yourself. It was a pity that towards the end you lost your head.'

'Lost my head!' exclaimed the Director. 'What do you mean, Pamplemousse? I was word perfect.'

'I was thinking of the moment when you were sent to the guillotine, *Monsieur*. I imagine the applause at the end must have threatened to raise the very rafters of the school hall.'

Monsieur Leclercq eyed him suspiciously for a moment or two.

'You really think I could get away with it, Aristide?' he said at last.

'As to the manner born,' said Monsieur Pamplemousse. 'All you need do is refrain from uttering a single word of French. Under no circumstances should you ever say *merci*, let alone *merci beaucoup*. It will give the game away. If necessary, you simply shout at those attending to your needs until they understand.'

He felt for his diary. Run with it, as Mrs Beardmore might say.

'May I further suggest, *Monsieur*, since secrecy is the order of the day, Véronique telephones this number. It will connect her to Taxis Canine. They run an ambulance service for *chiens*. It will enable you to leave this building accompanied by Pommes Frites without arousing anyone's suspicions.'

'Pamplemousse…' Monsieur Leclercq rose from his seat and advanced round the desk, hand outstretched. 'Pamplemousse, there are times when I don't know what I would do without you.'

Monsieur Pamplemousse glanced down at Pommes Frites, still struggling to take it all in. And there are times, he thought, when I wish certain dogs didn't look quite so lugubrious. It makes me wonder if I am doing the right thing.

* * *

'Do stop fretting, Aristide,' said Doucette, later that evening. 'You've been like a cat on hot bricks ever since you got home. That's the second Krispy Kreme you've had. You'll be making the door handles stickier than ever if you go on like that.'

'I know the Director,' said Monsieur Pamplemousse gloomily. 'And I also know Pommes Frites.'

In truth, he couldn't remember how long ago it was since they had been apart for any length of time, and although he knew in his heart it was for the best, it still didn't seem right.

'I wouldn't call Monsieur Leclercq streetwise by any stretch of the imagination. As for Pommes Frites, even now he is probably acting like a small boy staying with his grandparents for the first time – hardly able to believe his good fortune that they can be so gullible. I fear the worst.'

The words were hardly out of his mouth when the phone rang.

'Talk of the devil,' he said, holding his hand over the mouthpiece.

'Pamplemousse…' The Director sounded in a state of scarcely suppressed excitement. 'I have only been in this hotel for half an hour and I think I have struck gold…'

'*Monsieur?*'

'Have you ever come across a device for translating dog barks?'

Monsieur Pamplemousse was forced to confess he hadn't.

'It is one of the hotel's extramural activities,' said the Director. 'One of the conversational aids Véronique referred to in her notes. I have a DVD in my hand at this very moment…

'According to the wording on the outside of the box, it was invented by a Japanese professor who has made a lengthy study of over eighty different breeds, including bloodhounds. Apparently his invention first of all breaks the barks down to the breed of dog, then into their frequency components. The result is analysed and transformed into digital voiceprints, which are then converted into words on a small screen.

'He has also written a book on the subject. It is called *Boku-Inu no Subete wo Oshieru Wan*, which means "I, Dog, Will Tell You Everything About Myself. Woof!".'

'I didn't know you were fluent in Japanese, *Monsieur*.'

'I am not,' said the Monsieur Leclercq testily. 'It is all on the back of the box.'

'Well, Pamplemousse,' he said, after a short pause. 'What have you to say?'

'Does Pommes Frites know about it yet?' asked Monsieur Pamplemousse. It was the only thing he could think of on the spur of the moment.

'I have yet to apprise him,' said the Director. 'However, it is my fervent hope that he will greet the news with rather more enthusiasm than that shown by his master.'

Monsieur Pamplemousse winced as the slamming down of the hotel's phone broke through the quiet of their living room like a pistol shot.

'Would you care for a pick-me-up, Aristide?' asked Doucette, breaking the silence which followed.

Monsieur Pamplemousse had not one, but several large 'pick-me-ups' before he retired for the night. Consequently it took him rather longer than usual to regain consciousness when the phone rang for the second time.

Screwing up his eyes, it was a moment or two before he deciphered the figures 01.49 on the digital bedside clock, and several more before he finally made sense of what was being said. It was a man's voice, and it kept repeating the word *Estragon*.

He wondered if he had been re-living in his dreams the original message that had triggered off his involvement in the first place.

'Pamplemousse! Are you there? Answer me!' The voice at the other end changed its tune.

Monsieur Pamplemousse sat bolt upright in bed and came awake immediately.

'Monsieur Leclercq!' he felt a tremor of alarm. 'Nothing has happened to Pommes Frites?'

'No,' said Monsieur Leclercq.

'Thank goodness for that!' Monsieur Pamplemousse relaxed. 'So he is alive and well?'

'Alive,' said the Director, 'but not exactly well. I am afraid he has blotted his copybook.'

'Blotted his copybook, *Monsieur*?'

'Not so much his copybook,' said the Director, 'as the pavement immediately outside the hotel.'

'The pavement outside the hotel?'

'Pamplemousse, I do wish you wouldn't keep on repeating everything I say. It is, if I may so, an unhappy failing of yours. I have pointed it out to you many times in the past.'

'Whatever Pommes Frites has or has not done to the pavement,' said Monsieur Pamplemousse, as patiently as he could, 'it hardly seems to merit shouting "*Estragon!*" at me down the telephone at nearly two in the morning. Surely it can wait until tomorrow?'

'Unfortunately, Pamplemousse,' said Monsieur Leclercq, 'the answer is no! Matters have escalated since we last spoke. One thing led to another, and not to mince words, I have been placed under arrest.'

Monsieur Pamplemousse settled back down into the bed.

'Perhaps, *Monsieur*,' he said, 'you should try telling me exactly what happened, starting at the beginning.'

There was a long pause while the Director marshalled his thoughts.

'We dined well,' he said at long last. 'Rather too well as things turned out. I fear it may be partly my fault. Despite the fact that they are out of season, I ordered three dozen oysters, perhaps somewhat misguidedly in view of the hot weather.

'We followed that with *foie gras* – Pommes Frites had rather more than his share of each. In fact, he consumed both courses with such obvious relish I thought that with the aid of the Bow-Lingual his findings might provide interesting material for *Le Guide*. I had in mind a separate section at the end with canine comments.

'Unfortunately, the first two courses proved to be an unhappy combination. Either that or there was too much liqueur in the Grand Marnier soufflé that followed the cheese…we shall probably never know. Suffice to say that somewhere along the line something disagreed with him.

'There is a notice in the hotel lobby warning guests not to go walking in the Bois de Boulogne after dark, so after we had finished dinner we went straight up to our room.

'In any case I was anxious to strike while the iron was hot and begin testing the Bow-Lingual. Unhappily, as is so often the case with even the simplest piece of electronic equipment these days, the instructions turned out to be rather more difficult to follow than the picture on the outside of the box would have you believe, and I'm afraid it all took longer than I bargained for. Being without any watchmaker's tools, it was over a quarter of an hour before the batteries were installed. The screws were ridiculously small. They kept falling onto the carpet and getting lost in the pile.

'It wasn't helped by the fact that Pommes Frites began nudging me with his paw. When I finally got the machine working it was hard to know what he was trying to tell me. Most of the noises he was making appeared to be untranslatable, showing up on the screen merely as a series of asterisks, interspersed from time to time by the single word "walkies", an American term which I must confess I was unfamiliar with at the time.

'By then he was jumping up and down and taking the Lord's name in vain. There was a cryptic message to the effect that Jesus was in tears.'

'Jesus wept?' hazarded Monsieur Pamplemousse.

The Director could be very trying at times, but Pommes Frites was normally of a very amiable disposition, and it was most unlike him.

'I can't think where he can have picked that up.'

'Be that as it may,' said Monsieur Leclercq, 'since it was gone one o'clock in the morning I thought it could wait.

'However, Pommes Frites clearly had other ideas, so when he started attacking the bedroom door I put two and two together and rushed him downstairs.

'Then we had to wait while the night porter took his time over finding the key to the main door. We just made the pavement in time. In short, he wanted to go to the bathroom!'

Monsieur Pamplemousse sighed inwardly. The Director was certainly living the part. It was as well to humour him.

'Pommes Frites never does "going to the bathroom" on the pavement,' he said. '"Walkies" was a very circumspect way of putting across the fact that what he really wanted was to relieve himself of *les besoins solides*. It was a loose translation.'

'That was certainly the case,' said Monsieur Leclercq. 'By

then there was nothing *solides* about them. *Besoins liquides* would have been more to the point.'

'At least he hadn't taken the Lord's name entirely in vain,' said Monsieur Pamplemousse. 'He must have been very upset.'

'*He* was upset!' barked the Director. 'What about me? You haven't heard the worst.

'It so happened that a police wagon was going past at the time. They were returning from a nightly patrol of the Bois de Boulogne.'

'And they stopped?' said Monsieur Pamplemousse. 'I find that hard to understand.'

'Why shouldn't they?' demanded Monsieur Leclercq. 'Clearly I had a problem on my hands.'

'I say that, *Monsieur*,' replied Monsieur Pamplemousse patiently, 'because statistically, twenty thousand or so *chiens* leave ten tonnes of *caca* behind them every day of the year. It is, you might say, an unwanted gift to the city of Paris.

'A brigade of sixty *moto-crottes* patrols the streets, but they have their work cut out trying to keep pace with it. That being so, a law was brought in imposing a fine on anyone found allowing their dog to defecate on the pavement.'

'And how many transgressors have been charged so far?' demanded the Director.

'The last time I heard it was four,' said Monsieur Pamplemousse.

'*Four*?' repeated Monsieur Leclercq. 'In how many years? That is disgraceful.'

'If, *Monsieur*, to coin a phrase, your own charge sticks, it will now be five.'

'It is still disgraceful,' boomed the Director. 'I have no wish to be a statistic, Pamplemousse. Besides, what is a dog to do when it has to obey the call of nature? There should be special *vespasiennes* for them on every street corner.'

'I hardly think that would go down well with the public at large,' said Monsieur Pamplemousse dubiously. 'Think of the queues.

'The problem is the city doesn't have its own police force to enforce the law and the Police Nationale don't consider it a high priority. To put it another way, it is beneath their dignity. That is why I find it hard to understand why they stopped.'

'One of them wished to urinate,' said the Director. 'I think it must have been brought on by seeing Pommes Frites. Then, following an altercation when I protested at his unseemly behaviour, they arrested me on suspicion.'

'On suspicion of what, *Monsieur*?'

'Not being who I said I was.'

'Which was?'

'Hirem K Rosemburg. It was the name I used when I checked in. I'm not sure why, but it came to me on the spur of the moment. It has the merit of being easy to remember. For some reason they were unhappy and demanded to see my passport, so I intimated I had lost it.

'They then asked me what the letter K stood for and I fear my mind went blank.'

'With respect, *Monsieur*,' broke in Monsieur Pamplemousse, 'it seems to me the police have a very good case.'

'You sound just like my lawyer,' said the Director plaintively.

'You have spoken to him?'

'He is on his way over here even now,' said the Director.

'To the hotel?'

'No, Pamplemousse, to a police station somewhere near the hotel, which is where I was taken after they arrested me. Is it any wonder that I used the word "*Estragon*"?'

'Oh, la, la!' exclaimed Monsieur Pamplemousse.

'Oh, la, la!?' repeated the Director nervously. 'What do you mean, Pamplemousse? Oh, la, la?'

'That is Inspector Malfilatre's territory. He will throw the book at you when he gets to hear. He once broke a collar bone when he slipped up on a pile of *caca* outside his house. He has had it in for dogs ever since.'

'It is coming to something, Pamplemousse,' boomed the Director, 'if a dog who, to all intents and purposes, is favouring this country with a visit from the United States cannot have its motions without the person accompanying him being arrested. It was only circumstantial evidence anyway. I just happened to be holding the other end of Pommes Frites' lead while he was at it. If only it would rain. A good downpour would wash away the evidence.

'In vain did I intimate to the officer who arrested me that I am a close friend of the American President.'

Monsieur Pamplemousse sucked in his breath. 'Whatever you do, *Monsieur*, don't mention that to Malfilatre. It was an American dog that was the cause of his downfall. I understand it caused good deal of merriment at the time because it was a breed called a Shih-tzû.'

'Nevertheless,' said the Director, 'first thing tomorrow morning I shall issue a complaint at the highest possible level.

'On the journey to the police station we had to share a van with some highly unpleasant creatures, most of whom appeared to be Brazilians saving up to go to Buenos Aires for some kind of operation. Quite why they should be arrested for that I don't know.'

Monsieur Pamplemousse was tempted to ask what happened to *anonymat*, but that would be rubbing salt into the wound.

'Where is Pommes Frites now, *Monsieur*?'

'He is with me – looking very sorry for himself I might say. I feel I shouldn't have taken him down to dinner. I daresay he would have been perfectly happy with room service.

'He could have curled up afterwards in the basket you very kindly sent him, but it didn't seem right to leave him all on his own. I am hoping that once my lawyer arrives he will be able to sort things out and we shall be allowed back to the hotel. As it is…'

'*Excusez-moi, Monsieur.*' Alarm bells sounded in Monsieur Pamplemousse's head. 'Did you say the basket *I* sent him?'

'It arrived shortly after we checked in,' said the Director. 'A very kind thought if I may so.'

'Was there any kind of note with it?'

'None that I found. It was gift wrapped and addressed to Pommes Frites, care of myself. I simply assumed it was from you, Aristide.'

'Whatever happens, *Monsieur*, you must – both of you – stay where you are for the time being. Do you understand?'

'Frankly, Pamplemousse, it is now almost two o'clock in the morning and I do not wish to spend a moment longer in this place than I have to. It has been a thoroughly unpleasant experience and the sooner…'

Monsieur Leclercq broke off. 'Did you hear that?' he exclaimed. 'It sounded like an explosion. It came from somewhere quite near…'

'In that case,' said Monsieur Pamplemousse. 'Forget all that I said. I will be with you as soon as possible, if not before.'

'Where are you going now, Aristide?' Doucette's sleepy voice came from the other side of the bed. 'I thought when you left the *Sûreté* and joined *Le Guide* you would be free of such goings-on.'

'That makes two of us,' said Monsieur Pamplemousse with feeling. 'You live and learn.'

Monsieur Pamplemousse had hardly finished putting his trousers on when the phone rang again. Doucette gave a groan as he reached out for the receiver.

'I have been thinking things over, Aristide,' said Monsieur Leclercq. 'Don't bother coming in. I am sure Pommes Frites will feel much safer if we remain here for the time being. I shall, of course, stay with him to make sure he comes to no harm. We can pick up the matter again in the morning after I have spoken to my lawyer.'

'On the other hand,' said Monsieur Pamplemousse, relaying the message to his wife as he carried on dressing, 'you could say there is never a dull moment.'

'Aren't you coming back to bed then?' asked Doucette.

'Not just yet, I'm afraid, Couscous,' said Monsieur Pamplemousse. 'I have a few phone calls of my own to make first.'

'Tell me again,' said Mr Pickering. 'I like it.' Weaving in and out of the traffic heading west out of Paris, Monsieur Pamplemousse did his best to oblige.

'I like it,' repeated Mr Pickering when he had finished. 'The more I hear of stories like that the more I warm to the philosophy of Jansenism. If Pommes Frites hadn't been taken short he might not be with us any more. It must have been meant.'

It was a sobering thought.

'Another thing. Here we are in the midst of a major security crisis. On the other side of the Atlantic they have this horrendous paper problem, leaving them hardly knowing which way to turn, whereas over here, things are on temporary hold because of a small pile of dog's doings on the pavement. The only plus is that at least you Parisians have learned from past experience to look before you walk.'

'I doubt if Monsieur Leclercq would call Pommes Frites' motions "small",' objected Monsieur Pamplemousse. 'And he would certainly far rather you said "where Pommes Frites went to the bathroom" rather than use the phrase "dog's doings". He is deeply immersed in the part he is playing.'

'Message read and understood,' said Mr Pickering. 'He is absolutely right, of course. Americans have a lively command of their language, but they invariably draw the line when it comes to talking about bodily functions. Characters in crime novels seem to spend a great deal of their time wallowing in blood and gore without batting so much as an eyelid, only to become surprisingly reticent when the call of nature intervenes. Not that we English can talk. We still ask to be excused so that we can "spend a penny". We have never really wholeheartedly embraced decimalisation. As for "spending a euro", it doesn't have anywhere near the same satisfactory ring, I fear.'

'*Merde!*' Monsieur Pamplemousse gave his steering wheel a thump as a car in front of him stopped without warning. '*Soularde!*'

'Exactly!' said Mr Pickering. 'You French have a word for most things.'

Turning right into the boulevard de Grenelle, Monsieur Pamplemousse crossed over the Seine by the Pont de bir-Hakeim and shortly afterwards pulled in to a side street near the Musée du Vin, where the Director's secretary was waiting.

Introductions completed, he set off again. Following Véronique's instructions he entered the place de Costa Rica, turned up the rue de la Tour, took a left into the avenue Paul Doumer and headed in the general direction of the Bois de Boulogne and Monsieur Leclercq's hotel.

The streets in Passy were noticeably less crowded than usual. The continuing heatwave was affecting business everywhere.

Pulling out to pass a stationary delivery van, he glanced across at Véronique. Clearly, she had been crying.

'Onions,' she said briefly. 'I thought they might help. Not that a great many of the tears weren't real when the time came. I must remember to disinfect the mouthpiece on Monsieur Leclercq's telephone before he is next in.'

'Mission accomplished?'

'I hope so. I went into his office first thing this morning and did as you said.'

'How about floral tributes?'

'I made arrangements for those, too. The one from Monsieur Leclercq is in the shape of a bone. I didn't specify what sort. I pretended the people at the other end were being a bit iffy about doing it in a hurry. I was quite pleased with myself over that. The other tribute from all the staff is in the shape of a kennel.'

'Good girl.'

'I asked for them to be billed to *Le Guide*. It's a good job it isn't for real. Madame Grante would have a fit if it landed on her desk.'

'We must spare ourselves that at all costs,' said Monsieur Pamplemousse.

'It seemed strange to think that someone else might be listening in. I hope I made all the right noises. You don't think…?'

'They are tapped into the office telephone line?' Monsieur Pamplemousse gave a shrug. 'I know what you are saying. *If* they are, and they don't hear the other end of the conversation they will smell a rat immediately and it will have been a waste of time. But if they go quiet it will mean they have accepted your call at face value. In that case we shall need to look for alternatives. It *has* to be some kind of bug.'

'Monsieur Leclercq has always been very security minded,' said Véronique. 'He is practically paranoid about it, especially near publication time. He also had it done immediately this latest thing blew up. That's how I came to know what was going on. Not that he told me, of course. I simply put two and two together.'

'I should know, but who does he use?'

'It is normally handled by Phoenix.'

'They're one of the best in the game,' said Monsieur Pamplemousse. 'The first thing they would check up on is the telephone system. If they didn't find anything nobody could.'

Conscious that things had gone quiet in the back of the

car, he brought Mr Pickering into the picture.

'A little subterfuge,' he said, over his shoulder. 'Testing the system, as it were. As you know, somehow or other information has been leaking from the Director's office. It is a little too regular, and they are too quick off the mark for it to be double guessing all the time. So this morning Véronique made arrangements over Monsieur Leclercq's private line to have Pommes Frites' "body" picked up from the hotel and taken to a funeral parlour for onward despatch to the dog cemetery at Asnières, just across the river from Clichy.

'Hopefully, if they do bite, the news will also lay to rest those who would be only too pleased to see it happen for real. Time will tell, and they are not in the habit of keeping people waiting.'

'I get the drift,' said Mr Pickering.

'In short, we shall have to look for something a bit more sophisticated than a telephone tap,' said Monsieur Pamplemousse.

'Or simpler,' said Mr Pickering. 'Remember the hidden microphone the Russians planted in the Great Seal of the United States at their embassy in Moscow during the Cold War? It may only have been a one-way device, but it was worth its weight in gold.'

'Something like that,' said Monsieur Pamplemousse. He wondered about the picture over the Director's drinks cupboard. Did the portrait of Monsieur Hippolyte Duval, founder of *Le Guide*, conceal a similar device? Phoenix *must* have checked it. Anyway, to use the word 'simple' was stretching things a bit. In the case of the Great Seal, the microphone had been built into a giant dummy replacement. Such a thing wouldn't be possible in Monsieur Duval's case.

'Let's hope you are right,' said Mr Pickering.

'We must wait and see,' said Monsieur Pamplemousse.

Véronique gave an involuntary shiver. 'The horror of it all came over me while I was making the call. It was like a tiny black cloud passing overhead.'

'If they smell a rat,' he said, 'they will undoubtedly move quickly…if not…'

'What then?' asked Mr Pickering.

'We will cross that bridge when we have to.'

Slowing down as they approached the Director's hotel he had to admit that despite Véronique's qualms, for the first time in days he felt more cheerful about things. It was like being back in his old job again. At least they were initiating some kind of action rather than marking time, waiting for others to call the tune.

Seeing two police cars parked directly outside the main entrance, he turned into the hotel's car park. He had no wish to be recognised at this stage; there would be too much explaining to do. While he was finding a suitably discreet parking space under some trees, he found himself automatically looking around for some way of getting Pommes Frites out of the hotel unnoticed.

That, too, was quite like old times.

Perhaps the answer would be to slip out through a service entrance at the back of the hotel after dark, get into his car and not come back. Often the simplest approach was best of all.

The problem would be if the phone ploy hadn't worked and the hotel was being watched. In the end he might have to risk it.

Having suggested to the others they wait a few minutes before following him in – the staff were probably still a bit edgy and it might give cause for comment if they all went up to the Director's room in a body – he left them his mobile, promising to ring when the time was right.

'I understand it is the Presidential Suite,' he said. 'Top floor.'

'I expected nothing less,' said Mr Pickering. 'If anyone stops you,' said Monsieur Pamplemousse, 'say you are visiting a Monsieur Rosemburg. Hirem K Rosemburg.'

'Now that I wouldn't have thought of,' said Mr Pickering. 'The plot thickens. Thanks for mentioning it,' he added dryly.

Apart from the police cars, there were no other outward signs of the previous night's incursion as Monsieur Pamplemousse entered the hotel. Seeing an unattended lift with its doors open on the far side of the lobby, he made straight for it.

All was equally peaceful on the top floor. Setting off along the corridor, he passed an open door leading to a utility room. An elderly maid sorting through some piles of linen looked up and gave him a smile.

A little further along he stopped at a door marked 'Presidential Suite' and pressed the bell-push.

A sound remarkably like that of a large dinner gong came from somewhere within and a moment later the door opened a crack.

'Pamplemousse! Come in…' Monsieur Leclercq stood back to allow him entry.

If Pommes Frites had been feeling aggrieved at being abandoned, he didn't show it. Pure unalloyed joy was the order of the day as he bounded across the room. Forcing the Director to one side, he leapt up to greet his master.

'How has he been, *Monsieur*?'

'*Lugubre*,' said the Director. 'Until now that is.'

'He often looks lugubrious,' said Monsieur Pamplemousse.

'It is nothing to worry about. One way or another I think he has good cause.'

Monsieur Leclercq gave a quick glance up and down the corridor before closing the door. 'You are alone?'

'The others are waiting outside,' said Monsieur Pamplemousse. 'I thought I would make sure first of all that the coast is clear and you are ready to receive them. I take it the funeral people will have been?'

'Over half an hour ago,' said the Director. 'I am not particularly superstitious, Pamplemousse, but seeing the coffin come and go did strike me as an unhappy omen. Pommes Frites clearly shared my misgivings, especially when they began measuring him to make sure they had brought the right size should they be stopped. I hope you know what you are doing.'

Monsieur Pamplemousse fervently hoped so too, but he kept his feelings to himself. He would leave the problem of getting Pommes Frites out of the hotel on hold for the time being.

'I am surprised you haven't been asked to leave after what happened last night, *Monsieur*,' he said, changing the subject.

'On the contrary,' said Monsieur Leclercq. 'I have been upgraded. The powers that be seem only too anxious for me to stay on.

'Such a thing, they say, has never happened before. A bit of an understatement, one hopes, but there you are. Assuming American nationality has its advantages. They are convinced I shall be suing them for damages. I have to admit, I didn't disabuse them. Americans are, by nature, given to litigation. I said I was awaiting a phone call from my lawyer.

'I have also demanded a written apology.'

Monsieur Pamplemousse looked around the room. Some

people went through life falling on their feet. If the main room was anything to go by, it was even more palatial than Claye Beardmore's suite at the Pommes d'Or. The only jarring note was a large wickerwork hamper on a table near the window.

'I thought we would have a cold collage for our *déjeuner*,' said Monsieur Leclercq, following his glance. 'I trust there will be sufficient to go round.

'Mrs Beardmore telephoned to say she has been unexpectedly detained and may not be here on time, so we may have to begin without her. On the other hand, I have taken the liberty of inviting "a certain person" along later.'

'Someone I know, *Monsieur*?'

'You will see,' said the Director mysteriously.

'All this secrecy and skulking in hotels is getting me down. Normally I would be by the sea by now, away from all this heat. Already Chantal's suspicions are aroused. She is beginning to suspect the worst.'

'You haven't told your wife what is happening?'

'I daren't reveal the truth. I doubt if she would be able to resist telling her hairdresser – in strictest confidence, of course. It would circulate the salons of Paris like wildfire, a good deal faster than announcing it on the web.'

Opening the lid of the hamper he began rummaging around. 'I must say La Grande Epicerie at Bon Marché have done us proud. There is a half leg of ham on the bone from the Ardennes – there is no doubt all those acorns the pigs devour while roaming the forests do impart a wonderful flavour – a selection of *pâté en croûte*, *foie gras,* cold roast chicken from Bresse, quiche, a 1990 Hermitage *rouge* from Chave, fresh crab and lobster from Brittany for those who prefer fish – the champagne is in the refrigerator, along with some Puligny Montrachet.

'*Fromage*, *fruits de saison*s – Belrubi strawberries, Charentais melon from the Loire and white peaches from the Bouches-du-Rhône – butter from Echiré, homemade mayonnaise… Perhaps I had better put some of the latter items to chill for the time being. In short, all the usual things one takes on a picnic…'

They may be usual to you, thought Monsieur Pamplemousse, but he couldn't wait to see the look on the faces of the others when they discovered what was in store.

It was time he called them up. Leaving Monsieur Leclercq to carry on with his work, he picked up a house phone and punched in his mobile number.

'The problem as I see it,' said Monsieur Leclercq, when they were all gathered together, 'lies with Pommes Frites.'

He held up a box. 'According to the wording on the outside, it should simply be a matter of attaching a small bone-shaped device containing a microphone to the subject's collar, then reading off the translations of its barks from a handheld display unit.'

While he was talking, the Director followed the instructions, switching on a device not unlike a mobile phone.

'Testing…testing…testing,' he said, putting his mouth close to Pommes Frites' ear. Pommes Frites gave him an odd look in return.

'So far,' explained Monsieur Leclercq, 'I have not had a great deal of success in getting him to bark. Heavy breathing, yes…but by the time that reaches the screen it manifests itself as a row of asterisks.

'I have tried everything I can think of…crawling around the floor shouting "Wuff! Wuff!"…making meowing noises like a cat…but he treats it all as though it were some kind of game. He insists on licking me.'

'Pommes Frites isn't in the habit of saying "Wuff! Wuff!",' said Monsieur Pamplemousse, rising to his defence. 'And the licks are nothing to go by. He was probably feeling sorry for you.'

'Hmmph!' The Director handed over the display unit. 'If that is so, Pamplemousse, I suggest you disabuse him before we go any further.'

Monsieur Pamplemousse eyed the object doubtfully. 'I should point out, *Monsieur*, he is the strong silent type. He never barks except in the case of an extreme emergency. It is all part of his training.'

'Well, you must untrain him then,' said Monsieur Leclercq. 'Impress upon him the fact that this *is* an emergency, and it is *very* extreme. Tell him the fate of an entire nation may hang on his "Wuffs".'

'With respect, *Monsieur*, I doubt if "Wuff" has any meaning to a dog. To Pommes Frites' ears it is probably simply a noise rather than a word.'

'We shan't know for certain until he barks,' said the Director crossly. 'Here we are on the cutting edge of what appears to be a breakthrough situation and all we get is a negative response from the chief participant. It really is most frustrating.'

'If I may make a suggestion.' Mr Pickering looked up from another sheet of instructions he'd found in the box. 'Pommes Frites is probably used to people speaking to him in French, whereas most of the sample translations they list are American orientated. For example: "I know I'm cute, so what do I say?", "Go ahead, make my day!"

'Or, taking another at random: "Are you my friend or my enemy?". None of them are particularly germane to the problem in hand.'

'Are you saying,' asked Monsieur Leclercq, 'that if and

when Pommes Frites barks, anything he says will be in French and therefore untranslatable by the machine? If that is the case I shall add it to my growing list of complaints to the hotel. In the meantime it is possible I could get Véronique to have a French version flown over.'

'Of course, Monsieur Leclercq.' Véronique reached for her notebook.

'With respect,' said Mr Pickering. 'I doubt if that will help. I think animals get to understand the language of whatever country they happened to be born in, but when it comes to answering back they speak in a universal tongue.

'If it were otherwise, imagine what it would be like being a German dachshund and wanting to change your mind. The poor thing would probably choke to death on words like *Gesinnungswandel*.'

'Mr Pickering is right,' said Monsieur Pamplemousse. 'Pommes Frites has a larger than average vocabulary when it comes to understanding what is going on around him and obeying commands...'

'In that case,' growled the Director, 'why can't you order him to bark?'

'Because, as I said earlier, *Monsieur*, it goes against his training. It will need time, and time is precious.'

Monsieur Leclercq stared down at Pommes Frites. 'Would that we had some idea of what is uppermost in his mind.'

'I think,' said Monsieur Pamplemousse, sensing the beginnings of a tail wag, 'what is uppermost in his mind at the moment is the thought of going for a walk in the Bois de Boulogne. Either that, or he is hungry.'

'There is one thing you can be sure of,' snorted the Director, 'if last night's carry-on is anything to go by, he won't have need to go for a walk in order to assuage any urgent demands of nature for some time to come.

'I suggest we put the whole thing on the back burner for the time being while we have lunch. Mrs Beardmore can take pot luck. A little Ardennes ham may put him in a more receptive mood for new ideas.'

Monsieur Pamplemousse wasn't entirely sure about that, but he wasn't going to argue, particularly when he heard the murmurs of approval from around the table.

'For the time being,' he said, 'until we can find some way of smuggling him out of the hotel, I wonder if he should have any food at all? The one may well compound the other.'

'Do you really think we shall get away with it?' asked the Director, softening his tone a little.

'A little misreporting in the press about the principal casualty wouldn't go amiss, *Monsieur*.'

'That can be arranged,' said Monsieur Leclercq. 'Remind me to get on to the editor of *Le Monde* immediately after we have had lunch, Véronique.'

Véronique reached for her notebook again.

'Perhaps we can create some kind of diversion,' said Mr Pickering. 'We could leave an unattended item of luggage in the foyer. Having it blown up would be a small price to pay.'

Aware of enquiring eyes turning in his direction, the Director abruptly moved on. 'Even if we do spirit him away, where will you send him? A so-called safe house?'

'A safe kennel, perhaps?' suggested Mr Pickering, then sank back into his chair as he received the full benefit of Monsieur Leclercq's steely gaze.

'I think I know a good place,' said Monsieur Pamplemousse, hastily. 'One where he will be happy. But first things first.'

While the others were busy helping themselves, his eyes kept alighting on the Director's picnic hamper.

He wondered if the funeral men had left their measurements with the Director.

Pommes Frites wouldn't like it very much, but if he curled himself up and they sat on the lid it might be possible.

What was the name of the film that had been all the rage a while back? *Honey, I Shrunk the Kids!* He should be so lucky. The sooner the hamper was empty, the sooner he could try it out.

They would have to remove the microphone first of course, or make sure it wasn't switched on. Left in place there was no knowing what Pommes Frites might come out with, given the latest additions to his vocabulary.

'Would anyone like a second helping?' he asked hopefully, helping himself liberally to a cold collage.

'We must leave some for Mrs Beardmore,' said the Director reprovingly. 'Not to mention my other guest when she arrives.'

Suitably rebuffed, Monsieur Pamplemousse joined Pommes Frites in a corner of the room.

His friend and mentor appeared to be lost in thought.

The reason was simple. All too well aware of the fact that everyone else in the room was eating, Pommes Frites was also conscious of the fact that his master was acting very strangely, one moment giving him long, calculating glances, the next eyeing the basket of food. At one point he even took out his pen, holding it first one way and then another as he squinted at it. Clearly he was trying to tell him something.

That apart, Pommes Frites found the object fastened to his collar was beginning to irritate him. As far as he had been able to make out from the little he'd seen, it was bone-shaped.

Not a real bone, of course, or even one of those biscuity

ones humans sometimes paid extra for, thinking they were a treat. It certainly didn't help matters; rather the reverse in fact, for it made him feel even more hungry.

A few swipes with his paw soon dislodged it, and not before time.

Looking round the room to make sure no one was watching, he picked it up in his mouth. There was a crunching sound and several wires and a battery landed on the floor beside him, along with sundry pieces of plastic.

He eyed them with disgust. Batteries he knew about. They made things light up, but as for being food, they were definitely a 'no go' area. He'd once known a Pekinese who had swallowed something called an AA battery with dire results. He certainly hadn't shown a glimmer of light.

Pommes Frites pondered the matter for a long time, eyeing his master's fast disappearing helping of food as he did so. The problem was he had no idea what was going on in his mind.

Over the years it hadn't escaped his notice that when it came down to verbal communication, dogs had the rough end of the stick. It was, in many respects, a very one-sided affair. If he wanted to say something, no matter how important it was, as soon as he opened his mouth to give voice, he was told to stop it at once, and he had to resort to sign language: licking, or rolling over on his back with his legs in the air. It was really a very demeaning way of going about things, particularly in company. He'd often wondered what the world would be like if humans had to communicate with each other that way, although come to think of it, from time to time he'd seen some of them doing just that.

He had never added up the number of French words he knew, but over and above those, he was expected to understand several other languages as well. People often came up to him in the street, patted him on the head and said something totally strange, expecting him to know what they were talking about.

On one occasion his master had explained to him the man was someone called a Serbo Croat and he hadn't understood what he was saying either.

All the same, he always tried his best. *Par exemple*: take the French words *alors on a compris*. He knew from listening to Mr Pickering and others who spoke 'English' that in their country it had to do with something called 'a penny' falling, which meant 'now I understand'.

At that moment Pommes Frites had a sudden attack of *alors on a compris* himself.

It dawned on him that the others in the room actually *wanted* him to bark. Not only did they want him to bark, but they weren't going to allow him any food until he did.

Having decided what the problem was, Pommes Frites lost no time in setting matters straight. Taking a deep breath, he filled lungs to bursting point, then let rip with a whole stream of barks.

The result was both immediate and extremely satisfactory.

Most of Monsieur Leclercq's *paté en croute* landed on the floor as he leapt out of his seat shouting 'Eureka! Eureka!'

His master let go of his plate shouting '*Sacré bleu!*' followed by '*Nom d'un nom!*'

Véronique gave a shriek, and Mr Pickering so far forgot himself as to make the sign of the cross and say something unrecognisable in English.

Fired with his undoubted success, Pommes Frites closed his eyes and carried on barking for all he was worth. He couldn't remember having enjoyed himself quite so much in a long time. It was like being left alone in a butcher's shop while the owner was away for the day.

Gradually his barks were echoed in other parts of the hotel. First from what sounded like an Alsatian further along the corridor. Then came an assortment of other, lesser breeds as his call was taken up by more dogs on the floor below.

Meanwhile, the Director made a grab for the handset, peered at the screen for a moment or two, then began shaking it as though mixing a cocktail.

'What has happened, Aristide?' he cried, giving the object a whack with his free hand. 'Where are all the messages? Why aren't they coming through?'

Monsieur Pamplemousse pointed to the carpet. 'I am afraid they are not leaving base, *Monsieur*.'

'What's that? What did you say?' Monsieur Leclercq gazed at the remains of Pommes Frites' 'bone' as though hardly able to believe his eyes.

'Don't tell me you have trodden on it, Pamplemousse!' he boomed in a voice that reduced even its erstwhile wearer to momentarily silence.

As Pommes Frites' barking died away, Monsieur Pamplemousse became aware of the sound of banging coming from the direction of the corridor.

'I'll go!' he called, clutching at straws.

Fearing the worst, he rushed to open the door and found the room maid standing outside. Pulling it shut behind him as she tried to peer over his shoulder, he noticed her trolley and as he did so his expression changed.

There was a large laundry basket on top. It had to be meant.

'Would you,' he asked, 'mind very much leaving the cleaning until later?' He took out his wallet. 'You can leave your trolley here. In the meantime, we are very much in need of a basket. I will make sure you get it back.'

'That is not necessary,' said the lady, nevertheless performing a disappearing trick with the proffered note. 'We have many more. Just as long as you don't complain about the state of the room, that's all. I'm off home now. I have my own work to do.'

'I will still make sure you get it back,' said Monsieur Pamplemousse.

Somehow he couldn't picture the recipient he had in mind taking kindly to a basket of that size cluttering up the apartment. Closing the door after her, he returned to the main room.

'What is the worst thing that can happen in a hotel?' he asked.

'Being a room maid and finding a suite full of people when you want to make the beds?' suggested Véronique.

Monsieur Pamplemousse shook his head.

'Pastry crumbs all over the carpet?' said Monsieur Leclercq, eyeing his floor space guiltily.

Monsieur Pamplemousse shook his head a second time.

'Clients who check out without paying the bill?' suggested Mr Pickering.

'You are getting warm,' said Monsieur Pamplemousse.

Returning to the trolley, he removed the empty basket and placed it in the middle of the floor.

'The wellbeing and good health of the guests is, of course, top priority with all good hotels. Not because they necessarily care two hoots about the individuals, but because if anything untoward happens to them while they are staying, it can rebound out of all proportion. The worst thing of all is to have a guest die on them. It is bad for business. They will go to any lengths to hush it up; discretion becomes their middle name.

'In a hotel that specialises in looking after pets, the loss of a dog could spell disaster. Having a bomb is bad enough, but to have a pet die on them…'

Having first detached a piece of ham from the bone, Monsieur Pamplemousse lifted up the lid of the basket and signalled Pommes Frites to jump inside. His command was obeyed on the instant.

'*Assieds-toi, s'il vous plaît.*'

Pommes Frites' rear end disappeared from view.

'*Mort!*' His head followed suit.

'*Bon chien!*'

'Communication is all a matter of using the right words at the right time,' he said, turning to the others as he closed the lid. 'Now, if you will excuse me I must put through a call to the management.'

Picking up the nearest phone, he consulted a list beside it and pressed a button. It was answered almost immediately.

'I am speaking on behalf of Monsieur Rosemburg,' he said. 'Mr Hirem K Rosemburg.

'Yes…the Presidential Suite. I have something very sad to report…

'*Oui.* That is what all the barking was about…

'*Oui.* The Great Kennel in the sky…

'*Oui.* I know it is the second one today…

'Monsieur Rosemburg is of the opinion it is Legionnaire's disease…a fault in the air conditioning, perhaps?… The whole system may need replacing…

'*D'accord.* That will not be necessary. We already have a basket…

'The goods entrance… I will give you the address it needs to be delivered to…

'Place Marcel Aymé…that is correct, Marcel Aymé…the 18th *arrondissement*…an apartment block by the statue to Monsieur Aymé…the seventh floor…

'*Oui*, I think Monsieur Rosemburg will also be leaving soon…

'*Merci beaucoup, Monsieur.*

'Perhaps,' he said, replacing the phone, 'someone will give me a hand carrying the basket to the door. There are times when Pommes Frites can feel like a dead weight and this has to be one of them.'

'But that is your own address, is it not…' began the Director.

'It is where he is happiest,' said Monsieur Pamplemousse simply. 'And even if all else has failed and they are still searching for him, I think at this stage, home is the last place they will think of looking.'

He had to admit he could hardly fault the hotel on their speed and efficiency once the matter was in hand. They had hardly reached the door when the bell rang. Opening it revealed two burly security men waiting outside. Bidding the others in the room a temporary goodbye, he accompanied the men down to the ground floor by the service lift.

It was good to know that Pommes Frites was in safe hands. Monosyllabic they might be, perhaps out of a sense of occasion, but they were clearly good at their job. Taking the *périphérique* and coming off at Porte de St Ouen, it wouldn't be long before Pommes Frites was safely home.

Arriving back upstairs he relieved Véronique of his mobile.

'Now, if you will forgive me, I must telephone my wife and warn her…please carry on with your *déjeuner*. If I may, *Monsieur*, I will make the call in the other room so that I won't disturb you.'

'Don't be too long, Aristide,' said the Director. 'Something tells me we should eat all we can while we can.'

Monsieur Leclercq's words, half spoken in jest, were to turn out more prophetic than even he anticipated before the day was out.

In fact, Monsieur Pamplemousse made more than one call and it wasn't until he was about to hang up on the last that he heard a familiar voice coming from the other room. Opening the communicating door, he went back into the main room just in time to see the Director embracing a new arrival.

'Elsie…' boomed Monsieur Leclercq. 'You haven't changed a bit. You feel exactly as you always did.'

'Saucebox!' said Elsie. 'I could say the same about you.'

Seeing Monsieur Pamplemousse emerge from the other room, she detached herself from the Director's clutches.

'You 'aven't rung Ron yet, 'ave you?' she said accusingly.

Monsieur Pamplemousse admitted he hadn't.

''E's been on at me to give 'im your number, but I didn't 'ave it, so I rang Monsieur Leclercq on account of Ron said to tell you in person. He says it's urgent.'

'Tell me what?' asked Monsieur Pamplemousse.

''E thought you might like to know the real Mrs Beardmore is alive and well and living in Seattle.'

Had Elsie announced that another bomb had been planted in the very room in which they were gathered and that it was about to go off at any moment it could hardly have had greater effect.

'Is he sure?' asked Monsieur Pamplemousse.

'Sure as 'e's doing five years for being careless.'

It was Monsieur Leclercq who asked the obvious question.

''E left 'is dabs on some Selotape din 'e,' said Elsie. 'You know what? Never press your mitts down on a bit Selotape if you've got dust on your fingers. It's a dead giveaway.'

'Has he any idea who this Mrs Beardmore might be?' broke in Monsieur Pamplemousse.

Reaching into her handbag, Elsie produced a mobile and dialled a number.

'You can ask 'im yourself,' she said.

Preliminary pleasantries aside, the conversation was brief and to the point. Monsieur Pamplemousse had the feeling that Ron may have had his own reasons for keeping it so. Prison walls tended to have bigger ears than most.

'It appears,' he said, as he hung up at the end of the conversation, 'that he once shared a cell with a chef who had a crush on the real Claye Beardmore.'

''E was doing time for demanding money with menaces off one of the female customers using an offensive weapon,' said Elsie. 'To wit, a potato peeler!'

'That doesn't sound very offensive,' said the Director.

'It depends where you put it,' said Elsie darkly. ''Er wallet wasn't the only thing 'e was after!'

'You must let me know the name of the restaurant,' said Monsieur Leclercq. 'I shall make sure it doesn't appear, if and when we issue a guide to the United Kingdom.'

'Anyway,' said Monsieur Pamplemousse, 'the man Ron shared a cell with was so obsessed with Mrs Beardmore, he not only had her pin-up on the wall, he used to sleep with it under his pillow at night. Ron says it was nothing remotely like the person staying at the Pommes d'Or.'

'Satisfied?' asked Elsie.

The others hardly had time to absorb the latest bit of news before Monsieur Pamplemousse's own phone rang. It was Doucette, confirming Pommes Frites' safe arrival.

'He wasn't too upset by the journey?' he asked. 'I made sure he had some clean sheets to lie on.'

'He seems to have picked up a cold somewhere,' said

Doucette. 'He hasn't stopped sneezing since he got here. Either that or it's the chocolates you sent me. You know what he's like…'

'Chocolates?' repeated Monsieur Pamplemousse.

'Don't tell me you didn't send them,' said Doucette. 'They arrived by special courier about an hour ago. I haven't tried one yet – they look very expensive.'

It was yet another case of *alors on a compris*.

'Don't!' said Monsieur Pamplemousse. 'Whatever you do, Couscous, don't touch them until I get back.'

Pressing the OFF button, he turned to the others. 'Hold everything,' he said grimly. 'It is all systems go. The worst is about to happen!'

By the time Monsieur Pamplemousse reached the Pommes d'Or a warning had already gone out over the France Info radio news channel. Carefully worded so as not to alarm the public at large, but strong enough to deter anyone from touching any unsolicited chocolates delivered by hand as part of an introductory offer; it simply said there had been a production fault and to take the box to the nearest police station as soon as possible in case the contents got into the hands of small children.

No doubt more specific warnings were being issued to possible targets as a matter of top priority. In one respect at least, the other side had miscalculated, or events had forced their hand. France no longer adhered to the concept of the whole of August being set aside for the annual holidays. They were now much more staggered. A good example of that was the 16th *arrondissement* of Paris, where a good half of the population appeared to have taken off already.

Bonnard was huddled over his controls when Monsieur Pamplemousse entered the Security Control Room. He looked harassed.

'Don't tell me,' he said, glancing up. 'Whatever it is, I would rather not know. It's turning out to be one of those days. Following that bomb outrage the other night, there's been a miniature tidal wave of guests heading back to the States. Now one of our Trottinettes has gone missing and we've only just taken delivery. The manager's livid!

'You wouldn't believe it was possible. Seven riders took off this morning to visit Napoleon's tomb. Only six returned.'

'Strictly speaking,' said Monsieur Pamplemousse, 'I have to admit I am here in an unofficial capacity, but I need some information and I need it quickly. If necessary, I can go higher in order to get it.'

'*Pas de problème*,' sighed Bonnard. 'Same deal as before. I've already had instructions to help you in every way possible.'

Good, thought Monsieur Pamplemousse. Now we know where we stand. The Director certainly hadn't been idle.

Bonnard settled back in his chair. 'Forget what I said earlier. I'm all ears. What can I do for you?'

'The last time we met,' said Monsieur Pamplemousse, 'you said you could provide me with a blow-up of a man in the restaurant, but it wouldn't be of particularly high quality. Forget the lack of pixels. I'd like whatever you have.'

'Ah, the mysterious Beardmores. We were talking about them just before you came in.' Bonnard directed one of his subordinates to put the matter in hand. 'We had a sneaking suspicion that might be what you were after.

'As I said the last time you were here, they're a funny couple…there's none so strange as people. That's certainly true in the hotel trade. You see all sorts.' Monsieur Pamplemousse took the blow-up he had asked for and stared at it for a moment or two. Once again he had a strange feeling they had met somewhere before, but he had no idea where…

'You wouldn't like a picture of Mrs Beardmore while we are at it, would you?' Bonnard broke into his thoughts.

'I'll take anything you've got,' said Monsieur Pamplemousse.

He watched while the other reached for a mouse and moved a cursor quickly to and fro across his computer screen. Then he pressed the left-hand button and Claye Beardmore's face appeared on another display unit in front of Monsieur Pamplemousse.

'Why is the quality so much better?' he asked.

'Because it is on the Face Recognition security system,' said Bonnard. 'Not the cameras used by the kitchen. They are not really interested in people, only what's left on their plates.'

'Tell me about Face Recognition.'

'It depends a lot on how big a database you have and how it's arranged. Ours covers current guests and those likely to revisit. If they don't return in a year they get wiped. We also have records we can refer to of known criminals who specialise in the hotel trade: people with a history of break-ins, assaults on lonely females, confidence tricksters. It's constantly being updated.

'From then on it is a matter of biometrics. The use of certain measurements: distances between the eyes, shape of the mouth and nose, the physical relationship between them, that kind of thing. What is commonly known as spatial geometry. There's nothing really new about that. It dates back to Leonardo da Vinci's time. He was one of the first to study it. The eyes, the iris and the retina, are reckoned to be the most useful areas. Unlike the rest of a person's face, they change very little over the years.

'For it to work properly you need to have faces filling the screen, preferably straight on, level with the camera. Then the system can make comparisons with existing pictures on the database. Anything else and it gets confused. That's why it doesn't work too well in crowds – as yet.'

'How do you get pictures in the first place without the person knowing?' asked Monsieur Pamplemousse.

'Simple. We use what is known in the business as a "face trap". There is a moment at the check-in desk when people registering turn to face the clerk. The camera is in the wall behind him. Funny thing, there's a red light just where they need to look and most people do. They can't help themselves. The person at the desk momentarily moves to one side, pretending to look for something, presses a button, and, hey presto!'

'So why don't you have picture of Monsieur Beardmore, if that is who he says he is?'

Bonnard shrugged. 'His wife must have done the checking in. If you ask me, by the sound of it she wears the trousers anyway. Besides, nothing's perfect. In fact it's a prime example of the kind of blip that arises in the current stage of development. I guess the two of them must have something in common because he was one of those booked out on the Segway trip this morning and when he went past the security cameras it threw up a picture of his wife.'

Monsieur Pamplemousse stared at the screen and then at the blow-up in his hand. His mind had suddenly gone into overdrive. 'When I had lunch the other day,' he said, thoughtfully, 'my own database had a similar problem.'

'What else can we help you with?' asked Bonnard.

'Two things…no, three. No…make it four…

'One: when you said they checked in as Monsieur and Madame Beardmore, did they actually arrive together?

'Two: Is Madame Beardmore still in her room. If not, where is she?

'Three: Who was actually riding the missing Segway?

'Four: Where is it now?'

'Help yourself to coffee,' Bonnard nodded towards a machine behind them.

'There's some Krispy Kremes as well. Make yourself comfortable. It may take a little while.'

Not having taken full advantage of the Director's lunch, Monsieur Pamplemousse was grateful for anything going.

In the event he didn't have long to wait. Bonnard looked

slightly shamefaced when he called him over a few minutes later with most of the answers.

'Rule number one,' he said, smacking his wrist in mock punishment. 'Never take anything for granted in this business.'

'As for your first question, we struck lucky with the check-in. One of the girls was on evening duty at the time and remembers Mrs Beardmore's arrival because of her Zimmer frame. She said, "once seen, never forgotten".'

Monsieur Pamplemousse had difficulty in suppressing a smile. The girl had it in a nutshell. It was hard to fault Bonnard's enthusiasm for his work, but it didn't need a state-of-the-art computer system to pin-point Mrs Beardmore in a crowd. He could have recognised her from a kilometre away.

'She also remembers hearing her say her husband had problems with his luggage back at the airport and would be along later. She thought maybe he had ideas of his own for an evening on the tiles, for which she wouldn't blame him.'

'And did he turn up later in the evening?'

'I'm still waiting for an answer on that one. The girl I was talking to had to hang up. It was a busy period.

'Two: Mrs Beardmore isn't in her room. The room-maid says their suitcases are still there and there's a wardrobe full of clothes and various other odds and ends, but they haven't checked out, or at least if they have they didn't pay the bill. The concierge hasn't seen her either. They are paging her now, but so far there's no sign.

'As for the Trottinette: Mrs Beardmore made the booking, but the person riding it was none other than, guess who?'

'Mr Beardmore?'

'*Exactement*! And where is it now? We struck lucky again. Apparently they met up with the official Segway Tour near the Hôtel des Invalides. Their lot were returning to base in the rue Edgar Faure. Their ETA after a four-hour tour is normally around three o'clock. There was a bit of a mix-up and in the confusion he must have taken the wrong turning and gone off on his own…'

'Does anything strike you about the whole thing?' asked Monsieur Pamplemousse.

'One and one doesn't necessarily make two,' said Bonnard. 'As far as we know, nobody has ever seen the Beardmores together…'

'I think,' said Monsieur Pamplemousse, 'we are on the same wavelength.'

Bonnard gave a whistle between his teeth. 'You think Mr and Mrs Beardmore are one and the same person. It would figure. But why? Assuming it's a him pretending to be a her, rather than vice versa, what is he? Some kind of nutcase? It doesn't make the room rate any cheaper. So, he likes dressing up as a woman. Who cares these days?'

Monsieur Pamplemousse could think up all manner of answers, but it was neither the time nor the place to give them.

'Right now he is heading towards the Eiffel Tower…' said Bonnard.

'He has been seen?'

'All our Segways come with electronic tagging so we can locate them. At not far off five thousand euros a throw, we can't afford to lose any.'

'How fast do they go?' asked Monsieur Pamplemousse.

'They have two fixed speeds – either eight or just under fifteen kilometres an hour. They normally use cycle lanes or the pavement, so that's the maximum they are allowed to do by law. When you meet some of the people at the controls you can see why.'

'*Merde!*' It couldn't be worse. The whole area around the Eiffel Tower was a sea of people most days of the year. During the summer months it was at its worst. While Beardmore was still on the Segway there would be no problem, but once he'd dismounted it would be like looking for a needle in a haystack.

'I must go,' he said.

'*Bonne chance!*' Bonnard picked up on the urgency in his voice. 'I don't know what it's all about. You must tell me one day. In the meantime, leave me your mobile number and I'll be in touch if anything more turns up.

'You could try the police post,' he added, while Monsieur Pamplemousse jotted his number down before taking off. 'It's in the south pillar of the actual tower.'

'I know it well,' said Monsieur Pamplemousse.

Foot down on the throttle, taking full advantage of as many short cuts as he could, he reached the Parc du Champs de Mars in record time. Abandoning his 2CV on a pedestrian crossing at a point where the rue de l'Université met up with the avenue de la Bourdonnais, he ran the last hundred or so metres into the Parc.

On the way he passed three manacled youths being 'helped' into the back of a police car. Pickpockets must be out in force. That, in turn, meant crowds. It didn't augur well. He switched on his mobile.

Reaching the east pillar, he slowed down to a walk and his heart sank as he surveyed the scene. It was even worse than he had expected. Lines of tourists queuing for the lifts that would take them aloft for a bird's-eye view of Paris snaked their way in all directions. The queues for refreshments and souvenirs on the far side looked, if anything, even longer.

Hard-faced army patrols in camouflage battle dress, FA

MAS assault rifles at the ready, fingers permanently on the trigger, were making their presence felt. Their eyes were everywhere as they strolled slowly in groups of three amongst the crowd. It should have been a source of comfort, but it wasn't. Try asking one of them if they had seen a man on a Segway and he would probably receive a very dusty answer.

He suddenly realised how much he missed Pommes Frites. It was the kind of situation where he came into his own, lending an aura of quiet authority in the process.

He was about to make his way across to the south pillar in the forlorn hope that someone in the police station would be able to help, when his mobile rang.

'You're in the right area,' said Bonnard. 'It looks as though he's abandoned ship near the Seine – on the right bank near the Pont de l'Alma. The Segway has been stationary for the last five minutes.'

Monsieur Pamplemousse stood where he was for a moment or two, unsure what to do next.

It was all he needed. Apart from the close proximity of a Metro station and another entrance for the RER line nearby, there were at least four bus routes to choose from, heading in all directions. As if that weren't enough, it was also the boarding point for numerous *Bateaux-mouches* trips along the Seine.

A second call from Bonnard made up his mind for him.

'Your wife has been trying to get hold of you. I said I would let you know.'

Monsieur Pamplemousse had a momentary feeling of panic in the pit of his stomach. If Bonnard was correct with his positioning of the Segway, and Beardmore was looking to make good his escape on public transport, it could be a number 80 bus heading for the rue

Caulaincourt and Montmartre. It was too close to home for comfort.

He tried returning Doucette's call, and having received no response, set off as fast as he could to where he had left his car, cursing his lack of foresight. During the intervening time it could have been towed away. The authorities moved fast these days when they felt like it.

To his relief, it was still where he had left it. Jumping in, he headed for the Seine, eventually joining a stream of traffic heading north across the Pont de l'Alma.

Almost immediately he realised it was hardly moving, but by then he was beyond the point of no return. The reason for the hold-up became obvious when he eventually reached the other side of the river.

Seeing dozens of grey riot police vans parked on the far side of the Place de l'Alma, he turned off to his right down the rue Jean Goujans.

If Beardmore really was heading for Montmartre on a number 80 bus, he wouldn't have a hope in hell of catching up with it. Even allowing for stops *en route*, they had the advantage of special lanes for much of the way and the drivers made full use of them.

One passed him at speed soon after he rejoined its route in the avenue Matignon, another overtook him as he neared the Gare St Lazare, both drivers clearly making up for lost time. By the time he breasted the hill in the rue Caulaincourt and turned up the avenue Junot on the home stretch he was at his wits' end.

'Now you know how I feel when you disappear for hours on end and I have no idea whether you are alive or dead,' said Doucette. 'It's worse now than it was when you were with the *Sûreté*. You seem to attract trouble, Aristide. Sometimes I wonder why I married you.'

'Listen, Couscous,' said Monsieur Pamplemousse. 'It was for your own good that I didn't say anything before. You would most certainly have been even more worried had I done so.'

With that he gave Doucette a condensed version of everything that had happened since the evening of the storm, until the moment when she had told him of the arrival of the chocolates.

'Who knows what they contain?' he said.

'At least I know where they came from,' said Doucette.

'What!' Monsieur Pamplemousse stared at her.

'Pommes Frites showed me,' said Doucette. 'That's why I was out when you phoned just now. You really should listen to him more often, instead of playing around with all those toys and gadgets. They don't tell you anything someone with a *soupçon* of common sense wouldn't be able to guess anyway.

'After I phoned you I came back in here and Pommes Frites was going frantic. It wasn't just the attack of sneezing, he was jumping up and down, trying to tell me something. At first I thought he needed a *pipi* after being stuck in that awful laundry basket, but as soon as we got outside he set off towards Abbesses, literally dragging me behind him. We ended up at that little boutique I was telling you about. The madame who owns it is a Maître Chocolatier and she has a diploma from the Club des Croqueurs des Chocolat of France.

'She was only too willing to talk. According to her she was commissioned by an American millionaire to supply one hundred small boxes of chocolates to give to his friends on his sixtieth anniversary. Apparently such orders aren't unusual in the trade, and having not long been open she couldn't afford to turn it down, especially as he supplied the boxes and the packing.

'She was in a terrible state. She'd heard the announcement on the radio about there being something wrong with them and she's terrified about possible repercussions. The integrity of her business is at stake. Being a small artisan, she can't afford that kind of publicity. It takes years to establish a reputation and you can lose it overnight.'

Monsieur Pamplemousse listened in silence. His mind went back to the night it had all begun. He had assumed Gaston had been coming to see him. Now it looked more likely that he had been following a trail which had led him to the shop. He might even have tried to call in on them on the way back and found they were out. He would never know. It was a sobering thought. It also explained why Pommes Frites had become a target. Claye must have homed in on his immediate reaction to the chocolates and taken action accordingly.

'First things first, Couscous,' he said. Pulling himself together he looked around the room. 'Where are they? I must send them off to be analysed straight away.'

'In the refrigerator,' said Doucette. 'I couldn't stand Pommes Frites' sneezes a moment longer.'

While she was gone Monsieur Pamplemousse's mobile rang again.

'You are not going to believe this,' said Bonnard.

'Try me.'

'He's been arrested for speeding!'

'On a Segway. Is that possible?'

'I didn't tell you,' said Bonnard, 'but they come with a selection of keys. Black, yellow and red. Black and yellow are for the lower speeds. The red one takes you up to twenty kilometres an hour. That's above the legal limit on the pavement. I didn't mention it because we don't use them over here for that very reason. Being American he probably knew about their existence and managed to palm one before he left.

'I thought he was making unusually good progress.'

'Even so,' said Monsieur Pamplemousse, 'surely a warning would have been sufficient?'

'Not if you're a policeman and the person you stop draws a gun on you,' said Bonnard.

Monsieur Pamplemousse was late arriving at a meeting convened several days later in the Director's office. Having tendered his apologies, he took stock of the others.

Monsieur Leclercq was there, as was only to be expected, along with Mr Pickering and Véronique. Also present, rather to his surprise, was Elsie, looking bronzed and fit, along with a tall, elegant figure standing with his back to the light, exuding the kind of diplomatic charm suggestive of time well spent at *les Grands Corps de l'Etat* in his younger days.

They were all dressed for the occasion, and he wished now he'd given Pommes Frites a bath before leaving home – he was still looking bedraggled after his journey in the laundry basket, but it had been at the Director's insistence that he brought him along too.

'Firstly,' said the visitor, 'I am instructed to convey congratulations all round. In doing so I must point out that this meeting is strictly *sub judice* and is not to be discussed outside these four walls, now, or at any time in the future. As far as the outside world is concerned the events you were a party to never took place.'

He turned to Elsie. 'I shall be most grateful if you would pay my respects to your partner, along with our deep appreciation for the part he played, not only in the run up to the whole affair, but in regard to the vital information he subsequently passed on, which undoubtedly helped bring it to a happy conclusion.'

'I still don't understand how you came to be involved,' said Monsieur Leclercq.

'Ron sent me, din 'e,' said Elsie. 'There's not much on the grapevine passes 'im by. Proper walking information service 'e is. As soon as 'e got wind of what was going on 'e sent me over to check up.

'All it needed was a photo on the email to confirm what 'e already suspected. I don't know the name of the one who was passing 'imself off as Mrs Beardmore, but according to Ron 'e's as crooked as a corkscrew.'

'We were on a state of high alert by then,' said the visitor. 'There was a lot of information coming in. Almost too much.'

Monsieur Pamplemousse caught Mr Pickering's eye.

'Ron says 'e was born behind a roulette wheel and 'e's been going round and round ever since.'

'He was correct in many respects,' agreed the visitor. 'We have since learnt that he was born in Las Vegas. He began his working life as an electronics engineer cum spare time drag artist at one of the big casinos in the days when the Mafia ruled the roost. Having a foot in both camps as it were, led him in the fullness of time to a job with the FBI. Always a cross-dresser, his activities came to the attention of J Edgar Hoover and he received favourable reports, which stood him in good stead later on when he was taken on by the CIA. Unfortunately, he turned out to be the proverbial bad apple,'

'Like Ron said,' remarked Elsie, ''E was as crooked as a corkscrew.'

'I have no doubt that the authorities will look kindly on your partner's contribution,' continued their visitor, 'and perhaps even bring about a review of his present sentence. We intend to make suitable representations.'

''E won't like that,' said Elsie. ''E won't like that at all. Ron's very 'appy where 'e is, thank you very much. Rent free and all mod cons.'

'Perhaps,' murmured Mr Pickering, 'he could have his sentence extended.'

If the speaker was at all fazed by the interruptions, he didn't show it. He was already commending Véronique on the part she had played.

'And now, *Mesdemoiselles...*' an elegant bow indicated their presence was no longer required.

The Director, still basking in the reflected glory of those around him, rose to open the connecting door for them.

'It has been a great pleasure, Elsie,' he said, giving her a fond peck on both cheeks. 'I must say you are looking extremely well.'

'I've been playing boules, in I,' said Elsie.

'I reckon it's something Ron could take up. It would do 'im good to get more exercise in between visiting days. Might put a bit of lead in 'is pencil.

'You might not believe this,' she gave Monsieur Pamplemousse a meaningful glance, 'but I won my first ever game 'ands down and I 'aven't looked back since.'

Having got to know Bonnard, Monsieur Pamplemousse guessed what was coming.

'There's this rule that says whoever is on the winning team gets their backside kissed by the losers.'

'I always thought that was what you English call an old wives' tale,' said Monsieur Pamplemousse.

'More like an old French 'usband's, if you ask me,' said Elsie. 'According to the other team they've mislaid the dummy they're supposed to use, so they 'ad to make do with the real thing. They've all been at it. They're worse than Pommes Frites. Some days it feels like I've been sitting in a puddle.'

Monsieur Leclercq looked aghast at the thought. 'You don't mean…don't tell me, Elsie, you have been lowering your *culottes* in public…!'

'That's always assuming I 'ad any on,' said Elsie darkly. 'You'll 'ave to come to the Luxembourg Gardens one day and find out, won't you. I've been told it's my best bit!'

Turning to Monsieur Pamplemousse, she handed him a large brown envelope.

'Ron asked me to give you this. 'E says it's very rare, but you might like to have it to put under your pillow at night.'

With that, and a final flourish of her 'best bit', Elsie followed on after Véronique. Monsieur Leclercq hastily closed the door behind her.

'A one-off,' he said, breaking the silence.

After a suitable pause the anonymous visitor took up the conversation again.

'You could say our quarry was handed the whole thing on a plate while he was working on the Al-Qaeda problem. Violence begets violence. He happened to intercept a news item on the AZF bomb threats to French Rail and the idea came to him. Forget railways; why not strike at the very underbelly of France? Once the plan had been conceived, everything began to fall into place. A coded message to our security people set the ball rolling. Through his work, he already had his contacts in the milieu over here, and following 9/11, security forces the world over have been leaning over backwards not to put a foot wrong, so he was in business on both fronts as it were.

'His passport allowed him special privileges when he was travelling, and since very few people on this side of the Atlantic knew what Claye Beardmore looked like, posing as her was something of a master-stroke. It enabled him to throw up the idea of creating a so-called "think tank", partly as a smokescreen, but also as a means of providing him with a valuable source of information regarding the current thinking.'

The speaker directed his attention to Monsieur Pamplemousse. 'Thanks to Pommes Frites' and your own quick action, a major tragedy has been averted. Out of the one hundred boxes of chocolate that were sent out, a high percentage have been intercepted. The courier firm which, in all innocence, was employed to deliver them has provided us with valuable information and we are already homing in on others involved.

'For your information the contents of the boxes has been analysed and each chocolate had been injected with a small quantity of Ricin. As I am sure you know all too well, Ricin is one of the most deadly of poisons. It is stable and unaffected by changes in temperature. Also, it is relatively easy to obtain and there is no known antidote.

'Once again, injecting it into chocolates was a simple idea, but a good one. They not only look innocent, the vast majority of people find them irresistible.'

Monsieur Pamplemousse thought wryly of the way he had accepted one without so much as a second's thought. It had been a demonstration of how easy it is to succumb to temptation. All unwittingly he had provided an expert's opinion. He also remembered the medicine chest he had seen in the bathroom, fully equipped with syringes and all that was necessary to carry out the task.

The visitor turned to Pommes Frites.

'In normal times he would receive the highest award, the animal equivalent of a *croix de guerre* perhaps, but these are far from being normal times. Instead,' opening a dispatch box, he withdrew a parcel, 'we have a small present for him.'

'I think,' said Monsieur Pamplemousse, having seen the label on the side of the package, 'it will be more to his liking than any medal.'

'Finally…' Before taking his leave, the visitor turned back to Monsieur Pamplemousse. 'You may be interested to know that not all of the chocolates were injected with poison. One box was left untouched: the one which was sent to your home address. Make of that what you will.'

'Perhaps he fancied you, Aristide,' said Mr Pickering when they were alone.

'I think it was more likely a thank you for my advice,' said Monsieur Pamplemousse. 'After all, I did say what an excellent product they were.'

While he was talking he opened the unsealed envelope Elsie had given him and withdrew a faded photograph.

'Don't tell me…' said Mr Pickering.

'The genuine Mrs Beardmore,' said Monsieur Pamplemousse, holding it up for the other to see. 'And it is signed! She looks rather nice, although I doubt if Doucette will appreciate my having her picture under my pillow. I am happy to say she is certainly nothing like her understudy.'

'I can't picture him drawing a gun like he did,' said Mr Pickering. 'Surely he could have talked his way out of trouble and got away with a warning?'

'It just so happened,' said Monsieur Pamplemousse, 'that a demonstration by a group known as the Union of Militant Midwives was taking place in the Place de l'Alma on the other side of the bridge.'

'I wouldn't have pictured midwives as being particularly militant,' said Mr Pickering.

'They aren't normally,' said Monsieur Pamplemousse, 'but would you argue with them? Believe me, they may be small in number, but get them together in a group and they can be very *formidable*.

'In fact, there is only one thing more intimidating, and that is the CRS – the riot police; they are kept in reserve like a lot of caged wolves. There were vanloads round every corner, peering out of the windows, just waiting to be let loose… Seeing them all and feeling surrounded he must have panicked, and who could blame him?'

'All that for a few midwives?' said Mr Pickering. He looked sceptical.

'In France,' said Monsieur Pamplemousse, 'it is commonly accepted that the smaller the demonstration the more riot police there are in attendance. If it were not so, their Union would lodge an immediate complaint on the grounds that they were not being taken seriously.'

'Ask a silly question,' said Mr Pickering. 'I was forgetting the power of French logic.'

While they were talking, Monsieur Leclercq returned and began casting an eye round his office, opening drawers and rearranging his bookshelf. 'I still wonder how the information escaped,' he said. 'My only contact with the wretched person was the night we met up in the hotel.'

He began patting himself all over. 'Surely, he – or perhaps I ought to say she – can't have planted some device about my person while we were together?'

'It depends what you were doing, *Monsieur*,' said Monsieur Pamplemousse.

Glancing round the room his gaze alighted on the Director's desk and as it did so he had yet another attack of *alors on a compris*, the third in less than a week.

'With respect, *Monsieur*, I take back what I said. I suspect he has been in constant contact with you from that very first evening.'

Picking up the book on North American Indians Monsieur Leclercq had been presented with, he flipped through the pages. Drawing a blank, he felt the back of the spine, and having wormed his index finger down inside it, began ripping the jacket apart.

'What are you doing, Pamplemousse?' boomed the Director in alarm. 'Have you gone mad? I haven't even started reading it yet!'

He broke off as a mass of wires and tiny components were revealed.

'May I see it?' asked Mr Pickering.

He held it up to the light. '*Circa* 1960, I would say. This kind of thing was all the rage when the Cold War was at its height; a marvel of miniaturisation at the time, but a bit of a museum piece by today's digitalised standards.

'Bugs,' he said, handing it over to the Director, 'are rather like jokes. The old ones are still the best.

'A very satisfactory ending,' he continued, as Monsieur Leclercq left the room to show the book to Véronique. 'I suppose now I shall have to return home and make out my report.'

'What will you say?' asked Monsieur Pamplemousse.

'To those who ask what I have been up to, but have no good reason to know,' said Mr Pickering, 'I shall simply say MYOB.

'In the written version, which will take rather longer to prepare and will remain a state secret for many years to come, I can really let myself go. I picture heading it: "A Little Knowledge is a Dangerous Thing", perhaps followed by a sub-heading along the lines of "Every dog has his day".

'How about you?'

'I picture an evening at home for a start,' said Monsieur Pamplemousse. 'I have been away a little too much of late.'

He picked up Pommes Frites' parcel and weighed it in his hand. It bore the imprint of Boucherie Lamartine, 172 Avenue Victor Hugo. 'I think I can guess what is inside it,' he said. 'They are the finest butchers in all Paris. *Par exemple*, their beef is aged for a full twenty-one days.

'Doucette will be pleased. She was wondering what we could have tonight.'

'You couldn't, could you?' said Mr Pickering.

Monsieur Pamplemousse felt Pommes Frites' eyes on him. It didn't need a state-of-the-art electronic translator to read what was in his mind. Clearly, when it came to the important things in life, his faculties were still in good working order.

'I was just testing,' he said. 'The answer is, of course, no, not in a million years. But, who knows? Both Doucette and I like it rare and there is such a thing as "chef's perks". He may well let us have a taste for old time's sake.'

'Talking of tastes,' said Mr. Pickering. 'What do you think drew Pommes Frites to the chocolates? It can't have been the smell of Ricin.'

'Far from it,' said Monsieur Pamplemousse. 'They simply happened to be extremely good. Superb, in fact; on a par with those from Robert Lynx in the Fauberg St Honorè. They don't come any better.

'It just so happens he is allergic to the smell of cocoa. It makes him sneeze. The darker it is, the more he sneezes.

'Knowing Doucette's fondness for chocolates, he couldn't wait to show her where she could buy some locally.

'But don't tell the powers that be. They might ask for their steak back!'

FROM THE CREATOR OF PADDINGTON BEAR

MONSIEUR PAMPLEMOUSSE
Hits the Headlines

MICHAEL BOND

'MONSIEUR PAMPLEMOUSSE AND HIS
FAITHFUL DOG POMMES FRITES ARE
TRUE AND ORIGINAL COMIC INVENTIONS'
GUARDIAN

Monsieur Pamplemousse
Hits the Headlines

Michael Bond

During his time as an inspector with the Paris *Sûreté* Monsieur Pamplemousse had been 'in at the death' on more than one occasion, but even he had to admit that the phrase took on an entirely new meaning when he was present at the spectacular ending to *Cuisine de Chavignol*, France's premier television cookery programme.

Seated in the front row of an invited studio audience, he watched in silent horror as the eponymous host, having downed an oyster in close-up, uttered a strangled cry and slowly but surely sank from view behind a kitchen worktop.

Pommes Frites, sniffer dog extraordinaire, has his own views on the matter: Claude Chavignol was a bad egg if ever he'd seen one. Subsequent events prove him right, and soon he and his master find themselves caught up in a bizarre world of unrequited lust, murder and blackmail in high places.

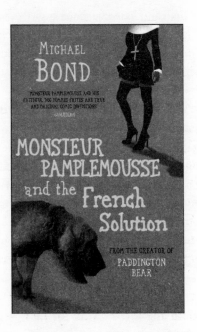

MONSIEUR PAMPLEMOUSSE
AND THE FRENCH SOLUTION

Michael Bond

When Monsieur Pamplemousse got an urgent summons from the Director of *Le Guide*, he knew that there was trouble at the top. His faithful canine companion, Pommes Frites, noticed it too.

But neither of them expected that the trouble would involve a nun who was in the habit of joining the Mile High Club or a full-scale smear campaign targeting *Le Guide*'s credibility as France's première restaurant and hotel guide. Someone has been spreading worrying rumours among the staff and infiltrating the company files – awarding hotels prizes for bedbugs and praising egg and chips signature dishes. Even Pommes Frites has become a victim of the assault.

It could all spell the ruin for *Le Guide*, but Pamplemousse is on the case...

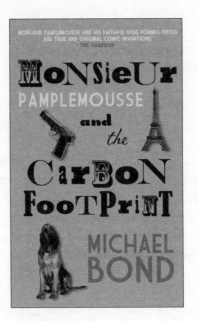

MoNSieUr
PAMPLEMOUSSE
and
the
CarBoN
FooTPriNT

MICHAEL
BOND

MONSIEUR PAMPLEMOUSSE
AND THE CARBON FOOTPRINT

Michael Bond

Le Guide, France's premier gastronomic guide, is failing to whet the appetite of its audience in America. Bribed by the Director with offers of some time off, Monsieur Pamplemousse agrees to flex his literary muscles in a bid to address the problem.

The result is the ex-detective's directorial debut, complete with walk-on part for faithful bloodhound Pommes Frites. Everything rests on special guest Jay Corby, acclaimed American food-critic, whose good opinion could change their transatlantic fortunes. But disaster strikes on opening night when a manoeuvre with a trapdoor causes Corby to storm out in a rage.

Monsieur Pamplemousse must find him before he ruins everything for *Le Guide*. Once again he can rely on star sniffer dog, Pommes Frites, who is hot on the trail of their only lead – the flimsy undergarments of an exotic dancer they'd happened upon in a state of undress earlier that day…

a&b

FOR SPECIAL OFFERS, LATEST PRICES AND
TO PLACE AN ORDER PLEASE VISIT OUR
WEBSITE AT

WWW.ALLISONANDBUSBY.COM

or phone us on 020 7580 1080.

Please have your credit/debit card ready.
We also accept cheques.

Postage and package is free of charge
to addresses in the UK.

*Allison & Busby reserves the right to show
new retail prices on covers which may differ from
those previously advertised.*